> **"Maybe I'll take you up on that haircut you've been trying to give me all summer,"**

Will said.

"I have? I mean… Yes, I guess I have." Much to her horror, Erica heard herself saying, "Sure, no problem."

No problem? She didn't know the first thing about cutting someone's hair. Hopefully he'd forget.

"Great, how about tonight, after the kids are in bed?"

He was so close, she could see the five o'clock stubble on his strong jaw, could smell the clean, soapy male scent, could feel the heat that radiated between their bodies. She admired the self-control her sister apparently had when it came to this man. She'd known him only half a day, and already she wondered what it would be like to kiss his seductive, crooked smile.

Dear Reader,

Happy Valentine's Day! We couldn't send you flowers or chocolate hearts, but here are six wonderful new stories that capture all the magic of falling in love.

Clay Rutledge is the *Father in the Middle* in this emotional story from Phyllis Halldorson. This FABULOUS FATHER needed a new nanny for his little girl. But when he hired pretty Tamara Houston, he didn't know his adopted daughter was the child she'd once given up.

Arlene James continues her heartwarming series, THIS SIDE OF HEAVEN, with *The Rogue Who Came to Stay*. When rodeo champ Griff Shaw came home to find Joan Burton and her daughter living in his house, he couldn't turn them out. But did Joan dare share a roof with this rugged rogue?

There's mischief and romance when two sisters trade places and find love in Carolyn Zane's duet SISTER SWITCH. Meet the first half of this dazzling duo this month in *Unwilling Wife*.

In Patricia Thayer's latest book, Lafe Colter has his heart set on Michelle Royer—the one woman who wants nothing to do with him! Will *The Cowboy's Courtship* end in marriage?

Rounding out the month, Geeta Kingsley brings us *Daddy's Little Girl* and Megan McAllister finds a *Family in the Making* when she moves next door to handsome Sam Armstrong and his adorable kids in a new book by Dani Criss.

Look for more great books in the coming months from favorite authors like Diana Palmer, Elizabeth August, Suzanne Carey and many more.

Happy Reading!

Anne Canadeo
Senior Editor
Silhouette Books

Please address questions and book requests to:
Silhouette Reader Service
U.S.: 3010 Walden Ave., P.O. Box 1325, Buffalo, NY 14269
Canadian: P.O. Box 609, Fort Erie, Ont. L2A 5X3

UNWILLING WIFE

Carolyn Zane

Silhouette

ROMANCE™

Published by Silhouette Books

America's Publisher of Contemporary Romance

To the Lord, for knowing me, and loving me anyway.

Thanks to:
My brother-in-law Bear, my sister's hero
and the Nutman in our family tree.

Acknowledgment:
Thank you, Karen, for Huck and the camping trip,
and Ray...for knowing navigation.

SILHOUETTE BOOKS

ISBN 0-373-19063-8

UNWILLING WIFE

Books by Carolyn Zane

Silhouette Romance

The Wife Next Door #1011
Wife in Name Only #1035
*Unwilling Wife #1063

*Sister Switch

CAROLYN ZANE

lives with her husband, Matt, their two cats, Jazz and Blues and their golden retriever, Bob Barker, in the beautiful, rolling countryside near Portland, Oregon's Willamette River. After ten years of producing local television commercials, she was finally able to quit her job, and begin writing full time. She and her husband keep themselves busy renovating their rambling one-hundred-and-twenty-plus-year-old farmhouse, which Carolyn claims, makes *The Money Pit* look like a day at the park.

Dear Emily,

How could you have done this to me?
Pretending to be you is proving to be a real pain.
You promised this ridiculous charade would only
last a few weeks, but it seems like it's been forever
and the situation here is getting out of hand.

The kids aren't exactly the sweet angels you
described. And as for their father, well you
certainly didn't mention how attractive Will is.
You claimed the man hardly knew you were alive,
so why is he always giving me those...looks?
Emily, Will doesn't need a nanny—he needs a
wife! And I don't think I'm willing to go that far,
not even for you, sister dear.

When are you coming back?

Love, (I think)

Erica

P.S. If I had any idea where in the world you were,
I'd actually be able to mail this letter.

Chapter One

The high-pitched whine of some mysterious Northern California insects serenaded Erica Brant as she struggled down the long, dusty driveway toward Will Spencer's old farmhouse. At least, she thought it was the sound of bugs. Perhaps it was the sound of her brain beginning to fry—it was hot. Shifting her massive suitcase from one aching hand to the other, she rested briefly in the shadow of one of the many shade trees that lined his seemingly endless driveway and cursed her bleeding-heart sister once again.

Sweat trickled down her spine and Erica wondered if it was from the terrible heat, or the terrifying jam she'd suddenly found herself in. Gripping her cumbersome load more firmly, she squared her shoulders, took a deep breath and continued her exhausting journey down the driveway and into the unknown world she'd taken to calling the "Nanny Zone."

"Damn it, Emily," she muttered as she stumbled over a large root. Balancing herself on the edge of one of her gargantuan suitcases, she rubbed her throbbing foot and tried to decide if it was too late to turn around, hobble back down the driveway, hitch a ride into the Podunk town of Harvest Valley and catch a bus back to San Francisco. She was a nurse, not a nanny. She didn't belong here.

How she'd ever let her identical twin sister fast-talk her into this mess, she'd forever wonder. It seemed Emily had always had that kind of power over people. The power to make the insane seem sane. The power to make the impossible seem easy. The power to make people think that her ridiculous ideas had been their own. Funny how, without Emily's stalwart reassurances that everything would be okay, Erica was beginning to panic.

"How am I supposed to pull this off?" she asked the cloudless blue sky.

And her identical twin sister's voice echoed persuasively in her head, *"Just pretend you're me...."*

Had it been only two days since she'd agreed to this folly?

"Emily Brant, have you lost your mind?" Erica dropped the Help Wanted section of the paper she'd been searching and stared in shock at her sister. "You want me to *what?*" As she peered dumbfoundedly at Emily's earnest expression, her worst fears were confirmed. Her overly sentimental twin was perfectly serious.

"It's only for the rest of the summer, not even the whole summer, Erica, just a month or two till I get back," Emily pleaded, her limpid brown eyes full of hope. Plopping down on the edge of her sister's bed, she grasped Erica's hand and pulled her down beside her.

Erica shook her head in disbelief. "Forget it, Em! We would never be able to pull it off!"

"How do you know? You haven't even heard the whole plan!"

When Emily's lower lip began to quiver, Erica groaned in futility, then sighed. "Okay, I'll hear you out, but that's *all*," she warned, and threw an arm up over her throbbing forehead. Studying Emily through half-closed eyes, she marveled at how anyone who appeared so much like herself could possibly be so different.

Neither of them looked the twenty-five years that, no thanks to Emily, they'd managed to achieve. With their large brown eyes, heart-shaped, gamin faces and generous smiling mouths, they were still regularly mistaken to be underage. They had in common a straight, silky cloud of light brown, shoulder-length hair, the same slender, almost boyish figures, the same sweet and loving spirit, but that was where the similarities ended.

Where Erica was tidy and organized, Emily was sloppy and carefree. Where Erica was calm in an emergency, Emily fainted at the sight of blood. Where Erica enjoyed jogging around the block, Emily enjoyed marching in a protest rally. How they'd managed to share their old Victorian apartment in the heart of San Francisco for so long without tearing each other's heads off, Erica would never know.

"I'm waiting." Erica was impatient to get this over with. She'd hear Emily out, give some sympathetic advice about seeing a therapist and get back to her job search.

"Well, it would be nice if you would at least try to keep an open mind," Emily groused, and drew her legs underneath her.

"It's open—it's open. Just get on with it." A sense of foreboding crept over Erica as her sister launched into her plan.

Rolling the Help Wanted ads into a tube, Emily smacked the palm of her hand and went for the jugular. "Okay, fact number one. Ever since Mr. Clemmins died two weeks ago, you've been out of work." Emily knew that private nursing jobs for sweet, wealthy old men were hard to come by and decided to take full advantage of the situation. "Fact number two." *Slap, slap.* "The deadline on my research project has been moved up. I need to spend a month or so working on the thesis for my doctorate in sociology. I've chosen the homeless as my topic and I'm leaving for L.A. on Monday to do it. Fact number three." *Slap, slap, slap.* "Will Spencer and his kids are counting on me to come back to Harvest Valley for the rest of the summer and look after them. Fact number four." *Slap, slap, slap, slap.* "You need a job, Will needs a nanny and I need to work on my thesis. It's perfect!"

Before Emily could continue pleading her irritating case, Erica bolted upright on the bed and grabbed the rolled-up classifieds out of her sister's hand.

"Fact number one," she mimicked, and hit Emily on her knee. "It is only a matter of time before I get another private nursing job for someone like Mr. Clemmins. Fact number two." *Slap, slap.* She whacked Emily's hands. "Going to live among the homeless is a crazy idea and you could get yourself killed. Fact number three." *Slap, slap, slap.* She hit Emily over the top of her head. "I don't know the first thing about being a nanny. Not to mention the fact that I don't even *like* kids. Fact number four. I'll find my own job, thank you very much, you have your head examined—and—what's-his-name can just go find himself another nanny." With one final, resounding bop on her sister's dismayed head, she smiled as if the matter were closed.

It wasn't.

"But, Erica, you don't understand! When I took this job in May, I promised Will that I would be there all summer. They've been through too many nannies already! Those kids need some stability in their lives." Emily pursed her lips at the suspicious glint in Erica's eye. "They're great kids, Erica. I can't let them down. As soon as I get back from L.A., I'll come back and take over until school starts, and you can come home and get a nursing job."

"Why don't you just call him and tell him that something came up? It's only the middle of July. Surely there is some fool out there who would love to go take care of a couple of kids out in the boondocks."

"I *can't!* When I took this job, he made me promise that I would be there all summer! Will *needs* me," Emily cajoled, gripping Erica's sleeve in desperation.

"*Will* needs you? I thought you were his nanny, not his wife."

Emily blushed furiously. "Well, someday, er, I . . ." she stammered helplessly, "I hope to be."

"Em . . ." Erica's eyes narrowed in suspicion. "What aren't you telling me?"

"Nothing!" Emily wailed morosely. She stood, shuffled to the window and looked out at the Bay, her shoulders drooping pathetically. "I think maybe, that I could be, sort of . . . falling in love with him."

Erica rolled her eyes. "Where have I heard this before?"

"I know, I know, but this is different!"

"I've heard that, too. Well?" Erica demanded. "Is he in love with you?" There was obviously much more to this story than met the eye, and Erica was getting nervous.

"Actually, no," Emily stated flatly, still staring stonily out the window. "I was going to, uh, work on that this summer. But now, with my thesis . . ." She trailed off in frustration.'

"Where does he think you are now?"

"I told him that there was a family emergency, and I needed to be at home with my mother. He was nice enough to let me go for the weekend. I'm supposed to be back on Monday," she said sighing dejectedly.

"Why don't you do your thesis on being a nanny?" Erica reasoned, racking her brain for an answer to her sister's latest predicament.

"No! This study I'm going to do is very important. I have a deadline, and I intend to keep it," she vowed fiercely, and turned to face Erica. "This research could someday save lives. I have to go!"

Searching her sister's tenderhearted face, Erica could see how much this plan meant to her.

"Em," she said gently, and rose to join her sister at the window. "You're going to have to make a choice. You can't be two places at one time."

"Yes, I can, Erica. If you would just help me out for one—two at the most—teeny-weeny little months, I *can*."

"Sounds like this guy needs a wife more than anything and of all the summer jobs I can think of, that is one I'm just not willing to apply for." Shaking her head sadly, Erica declined the honor. "Sorry, Em. But the answer is still no. Not in a million zillion years."

The sound of a screen door slamming brought Erica's head up and snapped her out of her reverie. Still perched on the edge of her mammoth suitcase in the middle of Will Spencer's driveway, she watched a distant figure emerge from the farmhouse and grow smaller as it headed for the barn. Will.

Erica shuddered. From the way Em had described this man, she knew she wasn't going to like him. Emily was always taking some lost cause under her wing. Will Spencer would be no different. Resignedly she stood and picked up the suitcase that threatened to tear her shoulder out of joint. She couldn't sit there all summer.

Trodding down the dusty lane, dragging her luggage behind her, she tried to remember what Emily had told her about old what's-his-face and his two rug rats.

As usual, Emily had painted an overly dramatic, highly romantic picture of the old coot, going on and on about how wonderful he was.

"Oh, Erica, he's so manly! He's about five foot ten inches, but you'd think he's bigger." *Um-hmm. He's fat.* "Thick, sandy brown hair, with just a hint of silver at his temples." *Yep. He's old.* "He's the strong, silent type." *He's grumpy.* "And he looks just gorgeous in his faded blue jeans and cowboy boots." *A geek.* "And he's so masculine!" she had gushed. "He has a gun, but he never uses it. It's just for protection." *Super. A grumpy old geezer with a weapon.*

Oh, well. If her flighty twin had finally met someone that she could love, then who was she to judge? No matter how strange this character might be. This just better not be another one of her numerous passing fancies. No, this had better be the real thing, or heads would roll. Maybe this time Emily would settle down. And maybe they were building igloos in hell, she thought acidly.

Well, it was too late now, she decided, as she reached the giant Spencer farmhouse. This is where she would be spending most of her summer, she mused, taking in the large wraparound-style porch, complete with a swing for two. The old clapboard siding sported a fresh coat of white paint, and stumbling awkwardly into the middle of the front yard, Erica set down her gear and stared in fascination. Appealing fish-scale shingles decorated the house's gable ends, and every window was flanked by two midnight black shutters. Darling Victorian gingerbread adorned the porch, spokes and spindles, corbels and doodads and flower boxes filled with bright red geraniums.

Behind the house, for what seemed like miles, lay acres of lush green hazelnut trees. According to Emily, Will spent almost every waking hour tending his orchards, preparing for harvest in the fall.

Good. The less time she had to spend in the presence of this curmudgeon, the happier she'd be.

"Hello, Emily." Erica was startled by the low, sexy voice that had come from directly over her shoulder. This was it. The moment of truth. An overwhelming sense of dread filled the pit of her stomach as she slowly turned to face what might possibly be her future brother-in-law. She let her eyes scan, with morbid curiosity, the man standing before her, and did her best to swallow a gasp of surprise.

Will Spencer was anything but a grisly old coot. No, Emily had been right. Will Spencer was quite possibly one of the sexiest men that she had ever laid eyes on.

"Hello, Will," she managed in an amazingly calm tone of voice.

He pushed back his Stetson and wiped his brow on his sleeve, smiling at her in welcome. Tugging off a pair of dirty leather gloves, he extended a hand in greeting and said, "It's good to have you back."

His relief at her return was obvious. *Just how rotten were these kids, anyway?*

"I didn't hear you drive up." He glanced around his parking area. "How'd you get here?"

As she took his strong, work-callused hand in her soft, clammy one, Erica could feel the strength of many years of physical labor. He tightened his grip, his hand communicating a brief message of curiosity.

"I took a cab to the end of the driveway, and I, uh, decided it was such a beautiful day that I'd walk in." She felt the heat steal up her neck and set fire to her cheeks. *He knows!*

Erica could tell by the way Will was looking at her that he'd figured out she was not Emily. His eyes probed hers with more than just a cursory attempt at politeness, and the intimacy of his look tied her stomach into a fiery web of knots.

Emily hadn't been kidding. This man truly was unique. Everything about him screamed male, and her first impression of Will Spencer was that of raw sex. And though he wasn't incredibly tall, or handsome in the classical sense, he exuded an animal magnetism, a blatant virility that no woman in her right mind could miss. His smile was somewhat lopsided, his upper lip curling lazily to show off a set of perfect white teeth, and his sky blue eyes had tiny lines etched by years in the sun. His masculinity was pure and unaffected as he stood, appraising her with sheer male appreciation.

Will broke the tension that radiated between them by picking up her ridiculous amount of luggage in his massive, well-formed arms. He looked at her in surprise.

"Do some shopping in San Francisco?" He didn't wait for a reply. "You shouldn't have carried this all the way down the driveway by yourself," he scolded.

Erica shrugged. He didn't need to know that she'd dragged it most of the way. "I didn't want to bother you."

"Don't be silly," he said. "It's the least I can do. Why don't we go inside, where it's cool, and you can freshen up."

Gesturing for her to lead the way, Will followed her up the stairs to the porch and through his front door. Setting the luggage down in the entryway, he watched her adjust to her new surroundings.

What was happening here? Will wondered, taken aback by his reaction to Emily. For the past two and a half months, he'd never really noticed anything about her other than the fact that she was great with the kids. Never really noticed the large, liquid brown eyes that flashed when she smiled. Never noticed her silky mane of shiny brown hair or the slender curve of those shapely legs, revealed beneath her gauzy yellow sundress. All of a sudden she was sexy as hell.

Removing his Stetson, he pushed the thoughts of Emily the woman to the back of his mind, and concentrated on Emily the nanny. Obviously the heat had given him brain damage. Either that, or he'd been without a woman far too long. For the most part, he still considered himself in mourning after the untimely death of his wife and infant son over two years ago. The fates had dealt him his hand. He was a confirmed bachelor now, and having played at love and lost, he didn't want to get involved. Ever again. It just hurt too damn much. He had no business being attracted to his children's baby-sitter. Feeling suddenly far younger than his thirty-three years, Will decided he'd better get while the gettin' was good.

"I'll see to your things as soon as I finish...what I was...working on out in the barn. You know where everything is, so..." His heart caught in his throat as she turned around, looking like a calf who'd lost her mama. Lordy, she was stunning. Something was definitely different about her. But what? Had she changed her hairstyle? Running a hand over his face to clear his mind, he said, "Make yourself to home." And with that, he walked back outside, the screen door bouncing off the heel of his boot as he left.

"Thanks, I'll just do that," Erica said with a sigh, and wondered where on earth her room was. She certainly couldn't ask Will. And just where the heck were his kids? She couldn't imagine being alone in the same house with Will for very long. Just the thought of that cockeyed cowboy smirk gave her hot flashes.

How had Emily done it? *Emily!* A light bulb burst on over Erica's head. If she was lucky, she might be able to catch Emily before she left for L.A.

Feeling a bit like Alice after she'd tumbled down the rabbit hole, Erica began a hurried search of the house. The living room was the first room she happened upon. The well-worn furniture and highly polished oak floors had the comfortable feel of an old robe. Braided rugs were placed helter-skelter, as were family photos spanning the years. Crossing over to the immense stone fireplace, Erica peered at pictures of Will and his family. The first portrait was of Will on his wedding day. His lovely bride gazed up at him in adoration, the light of true and lasting love mirrored in her expression. With her dark hair and almost translucent gray-blue eyes, she had the look of a tiny fairy princess.

"You must be June," Erica murmured, feeling a heavy sadness wash over her. Emily had mentioned that Will's wife had died in childbirth with their third child, and she thought that he still grieved and felt guilty over the loss of them both. *How sad.* Erica ran a finger over the dusty frame. The other pictures were of the kids. The boy looked like a miniature version of his dad, and the girl, unnervingly like her mother.

Afraid that she'd be caught snooping, Erica tiptoed away from the memories of another, happier, time and followed her nose through an archway, into what appeared to be the study. *A phone.* Hastily she dialed her home number. Emily picked up on the second ring.

"Where the heck is my bedroom?" she demanded at her sister's cheerful greeting.

"Erica? You're there!" Emily sounded pleased.

Erica snorted. "Yes, I'm here. Now, where is my room? And hurry, I don't have all day."

"Upstairs, first door on the left. Is Will there?" Emily asked.

"Yes, he's here, too," Erica snapped at the dreaminess in her sister's voice. "And I think he's onto us."

Emily's laugh tinkled over the line. "Nonsense. He doesn't know I have a twin sister."

Erica gripped the phone, wishing it were Emily's neck. "You mean to tell me you've spent two and a half months with this man and you've never told him you have a twin sister?"

"No." Emily grew thoughtful. "I'm sure. We never spent much time talking at all, actually. He's almost always out in the orchard. I think maybe he's hiding from life. June's death was a huge blow to all of them."

Erica was silent for a moment. "That's funny."

"What's funny?"

"Well, he seemed pretty happy to see me—I mean you." Should she tell Emily about the interest she'd noticed in his eyes?

"Really?" Emily squealed, delighted. "Maybe he's beginning to come around! You know, I've been trying to get him to notice me all summer, and so far nothing. But maybe he's getting ready to crack."

"Oh, for crying out loud, Emily! What if he cracks while I'm here? What then, huh? This is a heck of a spot you've put me in," she said in agitation.

Emily laughed. "Oh, Erica. You don't know Will. It'll be a long time before he's ready to look at another woman. Really. I know. All you have to do is flirt with him a little and keep him headed in the right direction. Dangle the bait, so to speak, and when I get there at the end of the summer, I'll reel him into the boat."

As usual, Emily had oversimplified. Will Spencer was not some poor trout waiting to be hauled into her sister's love boat. No, this man was more the shark variety. Dangerous. Powerful. Ravenous.

In frustration, Erica twisted the phone cord into a tangle. "Damn it, Emily! This is never going to work! I can't flirt with my future brother-in-law. That's kinky."

"Of course you can! Listen, Erica, for the past ten weeks, the man hasn't so much as looked at me. He comes in for dinner, eats and heads to the barn, where he stays till midnight. If the kids need him, they go out there. In the morning, he's up at the crack of dawn, makes his own breakfast and eats lunch in the orchard. That's it. Honest. You just have to take care of the kids. Sunday is your day off, and Will usually always takes the kids away for the day, so you'll have some time to yourself."

Emily paused and Erica could hear a doorbell ring in the background. "Look, Erica, I've gotta go—my cab is here. My plane leaves for L.A. in an hour and a half. You probably won't be able to contact me, so you're on your own. I'll call you at the end of the summer. Bye-bye, sis. Good luck."

"But, but..." Erica sputtered, the dial tone humming like a flat line on a heart monitor. She was dead meat. *"Damn it. Wait! You can't just leave me!"* Erica shrieked into the unfeeling instrument. Crashing it down in its cradle, Erica spun around, to find Will standing in the doorway, watching her curiously.

"Man troubles?" he inquired offhandedly. He hated himself for asking, but he just had to know.

"Uh, no...no...I don't have a...man," she informed him for Emily's benefit, and fidgeted guiltily. "It was my...mother. I...she...we, um, she's going away, and I'm worried about her, all by herself. We don't get along. We're very close," she explained lamely.

Will raised an eyebrow and grinned crookedly at her. "Oh." He was relieved there was no man in her life. For the children's sake, of course. It wouldn't do to have her mooning over some guy when the kids needed all her attention this summer. "The kids are over riding horses at the neighbors'. They'll probably be home in a couple of hours, so, once you get settled in you can start supper," he told her.

"Uh, sure. Okay. I'll just go unpack." She stood, watching him watching her, unable to move. He was still staring at her in that raw, physical way he had of turning her knees to jelly.

It was there again. The same heightened sexual awareness that had nearly bowled her over when she'd arrived. Hadn't Emily ever noticed? Why hadn't she mentioned the primitive animal magnetism that mesmerized her, rooting her to the spot?

His stance seemed relaxed, his powerful arms crossed casually across his broad, muscular chest, his legs spread slightly, planting him squarely in the doorway. But Erica read his virile body language and could sense a tightly coiled danger behind his lazy perusal of her body. She knew that she was in way over her head. He was far from casual about his nanny. Was this something new? Or maybe for the past couple of months Emily simply hadn't understood the passion that smoldered behind his incredible green eyes.

The ticking of an old grandfather clock roared in her ears, and Erica could feel the intensity of Will's gaze as though he'd reached out and touched her. They stood for what seemed like aeons, both paralyzed, both aware the other knew that something highly charged, nearly explosive, was happening between them. If this was Emily's idea of a cold fish, Erica wanted to know just what the heck she expected from a man. Did he have to drag her around by the hair like some caveman? As far as Erica was concerned, Will Spencer seemed pretty eager to jump into the boat. Too bad her sister wasn't here to see how nicely her plan was working.

"I guess I'll just go and unpack," Erica repeated feebly, and watched Will's glassy eyes refocus as he nodded.

"I'll get your things," he said, his voice taking on a sudden gruffness, and beat a hasty retreat back through the living room and into the entryway.

Erica followed him and wondered what she'd done wrong. He seemed upset, almost angry.

Inclining his head toward the old mahogany staircase, he said, "After you."

"Oh, no, after you," Erica insisted demurely, hoping he'd lead the way to her mystery room. "And please, let me help." She attempted to relieve him of some of her overly abundant luggage, nearly knocking him over in the process.

Her fingertips probed between his arm and one of her cases, and he felt himself reacting to her in ways he'd thought were long dead. The subtle scent of her perfume teased his nose and soft, silky strands of her hair tickled his arm. She was infringing on his carefully constructed space, confusing him.

"Emily," he groaned, straining under the load, "I've got it! You go first. That way if I drop something, only one of us will be killed."

Giggling nervously, Erica headed for the stairs. Touching him had been a bad idea. His arms were like tempered steel, his strength overpowering. She'd never met a man who affected her as strangely as Will Spencer did, and she was sure Emily wouldn't appreciate her sudden awareness of him.

Upon reaching the second story, she frantically tried to remember which door Emily had said was hers. Something about Will Spencer rattled the heck out of her. Was it the first door on the right? Taking a deep breath, she pulled open the first door she came to, and found a closet.

Will stood impatiently behind her, unable to move around her, and the closet door, to her room. "Looking for something?" he asked, attempting to seem nonchalant, as his muscles screamed for release.

"Just this," she said, beaming, and held up a tennis racket.

"You play?" He was incredulous. Emily? The dyed-in-the-wool couch potato? Since when had she taken up tennis?

"Not right now," she improvised. "But it's nice to know it's here if I want to." Cramming the racket back into the crowded closet, she slammed the door and said brightly, "Gee, it's sure great to be back!" As she pulled open the next door, she felt her smile freeze to her face. Damn. "Bathroom," she announced gaily, and felt Will's perplexed gaze follow her down the hall and into the first bedroom on the right. This must be the place.

"Just go ahead and set it down anywhere," she instructed, waving her hand airily around the austere, masculine room. "I'll unpack after dinner."

"Whatever you say," Will said dryly, grinning at her bold announcement that she would be staying in his room now. Though it was a nice thought, he didn't think his kids would ever recover from the shock. He was feeling a little shocked himself.

Why was he staring at her so strangely? And why hadn't he set— Glancing around the room, Erica suddenly realized her mistake. Mortified, she felt the tears welling in her eyes, and blinked rapidly to keep them from spilling. She'd been there only a few minutes and already she'd made a complete fool of herself.

"Just for a few minutes, of course, while I make space for them in my room," she jabbered blithely, staring in confusion at her surroundings.

Will looked so puzzled, she wanted to throw herself at his mercy and tell the truth, beg his forgiveness and then run for the hills. But she couldn't do that to her sister. Besides, she had a feeling Emily was right. This man needed a nanny. Fighting to regain her last shred of dignity, she smiled and explained, "I know it seems silly, but I've been wanting to organize my closet for some time now. And there's no time like the present," she chirped, and backed out of his room.

That seemed to satisfy Will. "Okay, then, have at it. I'll just set your stuff over here." And with a grateful groan, he deposited all five filled-to-bursting pieces of luggage on his floor.

Now that that was settled, he could escape from this shiny-haired, sweet-smelling, curvaceous nanny and go hide in a nice cold shower, where it was safe. He didn't need this aggravation. "Why don't you take a few minutes to freshen up and get settled, and meet me in the kitchen? I'm done for the day, so I'll give you a hand."

Where on earth had that come from? Will thought. For some strange reason, in the few minutes she'd been back, Emily had him so freaked out he was actually volunteering to help out in the kitchen. Amazing! When he'd interviewed her for the position three months ago, why hadn't he noticed how sexy she was? Will's eyes dropped to the slender curve of her neck. He might have thought twice before inviting her to share his home if he'd known she could have this effect on him. And why now? For half the summer he'd been perfectly safe, living in his own little world of emotional isolation, while she minded the kids. He didn't see any reason that should change now. If he had an ounce of sense, he'd go straight to the barn and not come out till fall.

"Thanks." Erica nodded. "I'd like that."

Chapter Two

Chapter Two

The moment Erica heard the door to Will's bathroom click shut, she raced down the hallway, searching for her room. It was, as Emily had promised, and she now remembered, the first door on the left. After a cursory glance at the Spartan room, she bounded down the stairs and paused in the entryway to get her bearings.

"The kitchen, the kitchen, the kitchen," she chanted under her breath, as she assessed all the various possibilities. The aging farmhouse was virtually filled with doors. "Let's go for what's behind door number one, Monty," she decided quickly, her heart beating wildly in her ears. "Coat closet, check. I'd like to trade what's behind door number one for door number two," she whispered to herself, her hands shaking as she yanked open her second choice. "Guest bedroom, check." *For the love of Mike! Where was the damn kitchen?* This house had more doors than a blasted hotel.

She could hear Will upstairs, whistling a happy tune in the shower. "Take your time, Will. Take your time." Erica drew

in a deep, cleansing breath and willed herself to calm down.
At the rate she was going, she'd be babbling away with the
other loonies at the asylum in no time. Door number four
led to the living room and study; this she knew. Door number
five was the front door. Ignoring it, she went for door
number six. Powder room.

"Oh, for pity's sake! Who ever heard of a house that
didn't have a kitchen?" Was it upstairs? Outside? "Come
on, lucky seven," she pleaded, and turned the knob. Behind the seventh door lay a large formal dining room, and
beyond that, the kitchen. Bingo. "Jay, tell her about her
prizes," she breathed, and doing her best track-and-field
impression, she hurtled through the dining room and into
the large, sunny, country kitchen.

What now? A frenzied search of the cabinets revealed six
cans of SpaghettiOs, a half loaf of green-and-gray bread, an
empty box of cookies and something in a plastic bag that
defied description. Just what did these animals eat?

A rude thunder vibrated in the walls, and the dull sound
of Will's shower ground to a squeaky halt. Damn. "Take
your time, Will. Take your time," Erica begged, and rushed
over to the refrigerator. Emily had been wrong. Will wasn't
a hazelnut farmer at all. Oh, no, no, no. He was a mold
farmer. For there in the recesses of his dank and rather
frightening fridge grew the makings of a first-class biology
lab.

"Oh, honey..." she sang, trying to imagine herself as
Mrs. Will Spencer. "How would you like your mold tonight? Medium rare? Poached? Fricasseed?" Her voice
dripped with sarcasm. Pulling open the freezer, Erica was
immediately engulfed in a heavy cloud of fog. Once the air
cleared, she was able to see what the Spencers had been ex-
isting on for obviously quite some time. TV dinners.
"Yummy," she said, as she attempted to pry one loose from
the stack. No luck.

Grabbing a knife and a meat tenderizer, she proceeded to hammer and chip at the freezer, to no avail. "And I thought hunting and foraging for food went out with the Dark Ages," she muttered, grinding her teeth in frustration.

"What are you doing?" Will asked, leaning against the doorframe and watching her in amusement. His thick, sandy brown hair curled damply at the collar of his clean cotton shirt and his thumbs were hooked casually through the belt loops of his jeans.

Erica jumped at the sound of his voice and wondered just how long he'd been standing there, watching her wrestle with their dinner. How dared he look so smug...so ma-cho...so infuriatingly sexy? "What does it look like I'm doing?" she snapped in exasperation. "I'm carving an ice sculpture for the table. The pheasant isn't done yet." Maybe he would fire her for insubordination and she could get the heck out before she made a real fool of herself over this man.

Taken aback by her uncharacteristic display of temper, Will threw back his head and howled. Erica grinned, liking the sound of his infectious laughter. He was so handsome when he laughed.

"Okay, so I didn't get to the store this weekend." His crooked grin was sheepish. "Why don't you go pick up a couple of pizzas from that little place in Harvest Valley, and I'll wait here for the kids? You still have plenty of time before they get back." He fished a set of keys from his hip pocket and tossed them in her direction. "You can take the truck, since the car is low on gas. I've got a couple of things I can do while you're gone."

"Uh, sure." Catching the keys in midair, Erica wondered what pizza place he was talking about. Where the heck was his truck, for that matter.

Seeming to read the direction of her thoughts, Will said, "The truck is by the shed. It's been acting up, so I'll be in the barn if you . . . need me . . ." His voice trailed off uncertainly as his eyes drifted to her lips.

What was it about her now? he wondered. It was almost as though she were a completely different person. The changes in her had been so dramatic, Will found himself thinking she must have met someone over the weekend and fallen in love. For some reason, the thought was strangely depressing. Why had she told him there was no man in her life at the moment? Was that why she appeared so nervous and disoriented? The cock-and-bull story she'd drummed up about her mother going away hadn't rung true. Had some jerk hurt her? She looked so vulnerable standing there, obviously hiding a painful secret. She seemed so lost. So bewildered.

Agitated, he clenched his fists and battled a sudden, overwhelming feeling of protectiveness toward his children's nanny. A feeling that was threatening to put a chink in his emotional armor. When she ran her tongue nervously over her rosebud lips, Will knew he should bolt. And why he didn't do just that was beyond him, for he didn't need or want to become involved in the nanny's problems.

Raising her lowered eyelashes, she met his gaze fully, her large chocolate-brown eyes full of confusion. Will could sense a deep secret lay in their depths and his heart ached for her. Whatever it was, it had her quivering like a trapped animal. Someone had really done a number on her.

Why was she affecting him this way now, after all these weeks? It was amazing that he'd never noticed her before, when she was obviously such a special woman. But then, it had been two hellish years, and he had missed June with every fiber of his being. Only recently had he been able to get through an entire day without feeling that he wanted to curl up and die. He shrugged, as though trying to shake off some mysterious power she had over him, and took a step back. Emily would just have to fend for herself. His life was

complicated enough without having to deal with yet another broken heart.

"Well," he said, and cleared his throat. "I'll let you get
to it, then."

Erica jangled his keys and smiled weakly. "Yes, I'd better get going." Too bad she didn't have the slightest idea
where. Following Will outside into the stifling summer heat,
she squinted in the painful sunlight and tried to figure out
which building constituted the "shed." Must be the metal-
lic structure with the rusty, rattletrap pickup truck parked
just outside. Will headed toward his huge red barn and Erica was on her own.

The old pickup truck's door shrieked in agony as Erica
struggled to pull it open. Heat shimmied out of its interior,
blasting her full in the face, melting her makeup. Dang it!
Was chivalry dead? Surely he didn't expect her to drive this.
Hauling herself up onto the filthy, springy seat, she stared
in dismay at the gear shift. It figured. Emily must know how
to drive this piece of junk. As she searched for the ignition,
she wondered absently how Emily was doing. Emily had
been the one born with the maternal instincts. She should be
here now, not wandering around the streets of L.A., homeless and penniless. If Emily were lucky enough to live
through this harebrained thesis experiment of hers, Erica
was going to kill her.

After a few sickly gasps, the old rust heap backfired a
couple of times and finally sputtered to life. Searching for
the correct gear, Erica noisily shifted through the box, much
like a java connoisseur grinding her morning beans.

Will rounded the corner of the shed and stood listening to
her effectively destroy his transmission. What was she doing? Crossing his arms across his chest, he stood scowling
at her, debating whether or not to offer her his assistance.
Noting the grim look of determination etched on her pretty
face, he decided to force himself to stay away and let her

work it out for herself. It was hard, though. A woman like her brought out his chivalrous streak. Today, anyway.

He scratched his head with his hat. Good heavens, he mused as the old truck groaned pitifully, one would think she'd never driven the stupid thing before.

Finally Erica was able to wrestle the truck into gear, and popping the clutch abruptly, she shot out of the yard and down the driveway with one last startled look of terror at Will. Grinning, he admired her spunk. Yep. Something was definitely different about that girl. And against his better judgment, he aimed to figure out what.

Erica turned off the faucet and dried her hands with a dish towel as she listened to Will stamping his feet on the back porch doormat. Dinner was almost ready, and still no sign of the kids. Should she be getting worried?

"Something sure smells good." Will sniffed appreciatively and ran a hand through his unruly hair, pushing it away from his face. An errant lock fell back into his eyes and he smiled self-consciously. "Maybe I'll take you up on that haircut you've been trying to give me all summer," he said, mistaking her worried expression for one of disapproval at the length of his hair. His eyes darted away from hers to the floor and back up again. "You've done a good job with the kids' hair so... I guess I can trust you." Walking slowly over to where she stood, he nudged her out of the way, picked up a bar of soap and began vigorously washing his hands.

"I have? I mean... yes, I guess I have." He expected her to cut the kids' hair? Worse yet, *his?* Darn it, Emily! She'd always wanted to be an only child, and when she was through with her sister, the homeless nanny-barber, she would be. Much to her horror, she heard herself saying, "Uh, sure, no problem." No problem? She didn't know the first thing about cutting someone's hair. Hopefully he'd forget.

"Great, how about tonight after the kids are in bed?" He smiled, reaching around her to the counter for a dish towel.

He was so close she could see the five o'clock stubble on his strong jaw, could smell the clean, soapy male scent, could feel the heat that radiated between their bodies. She admired the self-control her sister apparently had when it came to this man. She'd known him only half a day, and already she wondered what it would be like to kiss the permanent smirk curled into his seductive, crooked smile.

"Oh, well, uh, okay, sure," Erica agreed, exhibiting a confidence she was far from feeling. How hard could it be? After all, if Emily could do it, it couldn't be that tough, could it?

"Looks like you did some grocery shopping." Will eyed with surprise the bowls of fresh fruits and vegetables. "You didn't have to do that."

Yes, she did. She could barely find Harvest Valley, let alone the pizza place. Fortunately she'd happened upon the local grocery store, where, as luck would have it, Will had an account.

"Oh, no problem. Pizza seemed so...unhealthy." She busied herself pulling the pot of broccoli off the burner and emptying the boiling water into the sink.

Will realized his jaw was hanging open, and snapped it shut. Since when did she cook? And vegetables? Emily? The woman whose idea of a balanced meal was a pizza with four toppings. He was more convinced than ever that she'd been off cooking in some other man's kitchen over the weekend, and he didn't like it. Swallowing these unaccustomed twinges of jealousy, he moved to the kitchen table and sat down where he could watch her work.

"Mrs. Sealy called, and says she found those books you asked her about and for you to come get them when you have a chance," Will said conversationally.

"Oh, uh-huh." Erica nodded, searching her mind for clues to the identity of the unfamiliar Mrs. Sealy. Neighbor? Librarian? Mattress?

Will tipped his chair back and enjoyed the view as Emily bent over and checked the contents of the oven. Seemingly satisfied, she closed the door and picked up a damp cloth.

"Talked to Ted Barston yesterday," Will continued as she wiped down the counter.

"Oh?" She supposed she should know who this Ted guy was, too. Why was he doing this to her? Emily had promised her that he rarely, if ever, engaged in conversation with his nanny.

"Um-hmm." Will nodded, a feeling of domestic tranquillity beginning to thaw his frozen heart. He was suddenly enveloped by a happy contentment he hadn't felt in years. "Says we can use some of his camping gear for our trip this summer."

"The camping trip..." Erica said slowly, her brow furrowed in concentration. This was definitely news to her. Emily had never said anything about a camping trip.

"Sure, didn't July mention it to you when she came to pick up the kids for the day last month?"

"Something like that..." she answered noncommittally, and rinsed out the cloth she'd been using. July, July, July. That sounded familiar. Oh, yes! The kids' aunt. Practically panting from panic, she made a conscious effort to breathe more slowly."

"The kids were yapping about it all weekend. It's all they can talk about." As he sat watching her chop lettuce for a salad, he wondered if she even remembered that he had mentioned the trip to her last week. Must not have made much of an impression on her, he thought disgruntledly. One of the few conversations they'd ever had, and she couldn't even remember. He tried to ignore the stab of disappointment.

Erica viciously whacked a tomato in two with a cleaver. Why hadn't Emily mentioned this camping trip? Was she supposed to go? Probably not. It must be some kind of family thing. "I'm sure they'll have a great time," she said cautiously, hoping he'd reveal some clue as to whether or not she was expected to attend.

"Oh, yeah," Will agreed, noticing her violent attack on their salad with a raised eyebrow. What was with her? Had she changed her mind about going? The kids would be so hurt. This would be the first camping trip with their cousins since June had died, and they were wild with anticipation. She had to go—he needed her to help keep an eye on the kids. And for some compelling reason, it was suddenly very important to him that she go with them. With him. He silently berated himself for trying to imagine that willowy body in a bikini.

The back door slammed shut and Erica froze midchop.

The kids were home.

Bracing herself for yet another identity crisis, she turned to face them as they tumbled into the kitchen.

"Hi, Em," Will's daughter greeted her breezily, and kissed her father on her way through the room. "I have to call Melodie," she announced, and disappeared.

"Hi, Sam," Erica called after her, breathing a sigh of relief. One down and one to go. According to Emily, thirteen-year- old Samantha had a phone permanently glued to the side of her head, and was no trouble to look after for this reason. Well, that would have to change, Erica mused, watching the pretty, albeit plump, version of her mother rush off to make her call. It was dinnertime, for heaven's sake. The phone could wait.

"Hey, Em," nine-year-old Danny called, and high-fived his dad. "Hey, Dad." He grinned at his father, his thick, sandy hair and stocky, well-built frame just like Will's. He followed his sister to the family room.

Swirling emotions warred for dominance in Erica's mind. On the one hand, she was relieved that the kids had chosen not to scrutinize her. On the other hand, she was outraged by their rude, offhanded attitude. After all, she hadn't seen them for two days. Well, actually, she'd never laid eyes on them before now, but they sure as heck didn't know that. She could feel Will watching her with interest, and attempted to reign in her temper. He seemed oblivious to their bad manners.

Smiling stiffly, she crossed over to the table and placed the salad in front of him. "I'll just go get the kids," she informed him, her back rigid with determination.

Will ran his fingers through his shaggy locks and scratched the top of his head as she bustled out the door. She was really cute when she was mad. Although just what she was so fired up about was beyond him.

Erica followed the sound of the blaring television set to the family room. There Danny lay sprawled on the floor, channel-surfing with the remote like the Big Kahuna of video. Samantha was lying on the couch, the phone balanced precariously on her plump stomach as she gabbed a mile a minute with her friend Melodie.

Sensing Erica's presence in the doorway, they both looked up expectantly.

"Dinner's ready," she told them. "Time to wash up."

The two looked at each other in surprise, then Sam asked her friend to hang on. "Just bring it in here," she ordered Erica, and giggled at something Melodie said. Danny nodded and turned his attention back to the television.

Erica couldn't believe their cavalier attitudes. *Just bring it in here?* Did they think she was their slave? Had Emily put up with this nonsense? Probably, she fumed, as Danny clicked from one program to another, then landed with interest on a particularly violent movie. Striding over to him, she snatched the remote from his hand and switched off the

TV. "You shouldn't be watching that," she chided the stunned boy, and turning with authority to his sister, reached for the phone and spoke to the giggling Melodie.

"Melodie, this is er, Emily. Sam has to go eat dinner now. She will be happy to call you back later. Bye-bye," she said, cutting off the sputtering teen, and hung up.

Sam's face was red with fury. "*Em!* Why'd you do that?" she cried, springing off the couch.

"Because it's time for dinner—that's why. Go wash up. Now," she ordered, and marched determinedly back to the kitchen.

"Daaaad!" Sam whined, rushing to where her father sat at the table Erica had set for four. Danny was hot on her heels, eager to see how his dad would handle this new turn of events. Em had always let them eat in the family room.

"Em says we have to eat in *here!*" she spit disdainfully. "And she hung up on Melodie! I could just *die!*"

"Better do as she says, then," Will said calmly, loading his plate with salad. "Go wash up."

Erica shot Will a grateful look and went to the oven to get the roast chicken, baked potatoes and whole-wheat rolls.

Scowling, Sam flounced over to the sink and stuck her hands under the faucet for the obligatory rinse. Danny followed suit, enjoying his sister's outburst.

"Come on, now." Herding the kids to the table, Erica did her best to sound perky.

Will's expression was one of dubious admiration as she loaded his children's plates with vegetables. This should be interesting.

"What's *this?*" Sam moaned pitifully, staring at the pile of broccoli on her plate.

"Eat it. It's good for you." Erica bit her tongue to keep from adding that the young girl could stand to lose a few pounds. It had been a long, grueling day, and she was in no mood to argue.

"This sucks," Sam griped. "You never used to torture us with broccoli before." She stared at Erica as if seeing her for the first time.

Well, if this didn't get her fired, nothing would, Erica thought, and slammed her serving dish down on the table, startling the entire Spencer family.

"I'll thank you to watch your mouth, young lady. There are people out there who have nothing at all to eat. People who are starving to death. People who would get down on their knees and thank the good Lord for this meal. Now *eat!*" she commanded the subdued child, earning a pair of matching grins from both father and son. All three members of her new family dutifully picked up their forks and dug into the meal she had prepared.

Will stifled a chuckle at her tirade. At least she was still preaching about the homeless. That much was familiar.

They all ate in silence for a while, the atmosphere strained to the point of bursting. Mentally calling herself every kind of fool, Erica kept her head down and grimly plowed through her meal.

Too bad Emily hadn't believed her when she'd told her how intolerant she was of bad manners. She'd blown it now. The kids hated her. "Emily the pushover" had probably let them get away with murder for the past ten weeks, she thought, glancing at Sam's unhappy face. The child looked absolutely miserable, her cheeks puffed out to avoid contact with the distasteful vegetables. If she knew her sister, Emily had been feeding them fast food. Healthy menus weren't exactly her twin's strong suit.

Will caught her eye and winked lazily at her, and Erica's flagging confidence was bolstered a notch. At least Will was on her side. But then again, considering how her heart raced at the innocent gesture, maybe that wasn't such a good thing. "Why don't you guys tell Emily what you got for the camping trip this weekend?" Will suggested in an effort to break the ice.

Danny tore the chicken bone he'd been gnawing on out of his mouth and turned to Erica, his eyes shining with excitement. "We got a new, really huge tent," he boasted, apparently forgiving her for turning off his R-rated movie. "All us kids will stay in it, and you and Dad can have our old tents. Aunt July and Uncle Charlie have their own."

Well, that explained that. She *was* going camping. But when? Where? "Wow, that's great," she said, struggling for authentic enthusiasm. She'd never enjoyed camping, preferring the comfort of a soft bed and working blow dryer to the inconvenience of the wilds. "Have you started packing yet?" That seemed like a safe-enough question.

"Not till next week," he mumbled around a mouthful of food. "Dad says I can bring my BB gun." He grinned with happiness.

"That's...nice," she chirped brightly, and turned to Sam. "What about you, Sam? What will you bring?"

Sam looked warily at Erica, as though not completely trusting this new, militant version of her nanny. "I don't know," she said, pushing her broccoli around on her plate. "We have two weeks before we leave." She looked up hopefully at Erica. "Maybe we can go to the mall before we leave and get...some stuff," she suggested, and flushed under her father's interested eyes.

"That sounds like fun," Erica agreed, smiling. She wondered what the child could possibly want that had her blushing such an intense shade of crimson.

"I'm done," Danny announced, as he stood to leave.

"Where do you think you're going?" Erica asked, her eyes narrowing at his half-eaten dinner.

"To watch TV," he said with a shrug, as though she should know this obvious bit of information.

"Oh, no, you're not. Not until you've cleaned your plate and helped your sister with the dishes." Erica knew that a cleaning woman came in twice a week during the school year, but school was out now, and there was no reason these two lazy lumps couldn't give her an occasional hand.

Slumping back down in his chair, Danny sighed noisily, picked up his fork and began shoveling his food into his mouth. Samantha was not so compliant as she looked to her father for support.

"*We* have to do the dishes? Since when?" Dismay at her ruined summer was written all over her face.

Erica bristled at the way the children always turned to their father for the final word when she'd already told them what to do. She was being paid to do a job and she was going to do it. Her brown eyes snapping, she issued the final word on the subject. "Sam, I feel that you two are old enough to help out around here now. Starting with the dishes, tonight. Is that clear?"

Sam glanced at her father, saw him grinning broadly, and shrugged angrily. "I guess," she mumbled.

Taking a deep breath to still her shaking hands, Erica nodded curtly at the sullen girl. "Good. I'll be out on the porch, if you need me." And with that she stood, poured herself a glass of iced tea and excused herself from the room."

The sun was beginning to set, and Erica couldn't decide if it was laziness or fear that kept her there on the old porch swing. The angry clatter of pots and pans being scrubbed and dried wafted out into the otherwise-peaceful evening, reminding her of the long summer that lay ahead. She was just in the process of wondering how she could gracefully bow out of this charade, when the screen door squeaked open.

Ambling across the wooden planks that made up the front porch, Will held out a pitcher of iced tea and cocked an inquisitive eyebrow.

"Thought maybe you could use a refill," he offered, and taking the glass out of her hand, filled it to the top. Hand-ing it back, he set the pitcher down on the floor and joined her on the swing. "You're right," he commented, pushing at the porch railing with the heel of his boot, which set the swing into a gentle, rhythmic motion.

"About what?" she asked, and held the frosty glass of tea up to her neck. Droplets of water dripped off the bottom of the glass and onto her chest, dampening the front of her pale yellow sundress.

"It's time. I've babied the kids long enough. They're strong again. It's time to get beyond the loss and get on with life." Pushing his Stetson back, he favored her with one of his alluring, slightly off-kilter smiles. "I've known it for a while now, but I just never seem to be able to follow through. June would never have stood for half the crap I let 'em pull. I guess I forgot about that. Till tonight."

The setting sun backlit Will with a heavenly light, bathing him in its iridescent glow. There was something magical about the moment, Erica thought, as she sat studying his strong profile. His wonderful thick hair was golden in this light, and his features were well defined and handsome in a rugged, outdoorsy way. She couldn't imagine him owning a suit, but she guessed he'd probably look great in one. However, he looked perfect in his well-worn jeans and the faded, plaid flannel shirt that stretched tautly over the gentle curves of his powerful build.

His expression was pensive, nearly brooding, and Erica found herself wondering if it was also time for Will. Time to get beyond his loss. Time to get on with his life. As if he knew what was going on inside her mind, Will turned his troubled gaze to Erica, and she caught a brief glimpse of the inner battle he was fighting.

For reasons he would never be able to understand, Will suddenly felt like confiding in her. "I'm going to try to be around more this summer, to help with the kids and all," he said, shifting his eyes back out to the horizon. "For the past few months, I know I haven't been much help, and I'm sorry about that. It's just that the orchards needed a lot of work, and I couldn't seem to deal...with..." He ran a tired hand across his jaw and shook his head as though searching for the right words. "Everything. I know they run wild without a mother. It's my fault. I guess I haven't been much of a father lately."

Erica murmured in disagreement. It was apparent to her that Will loved his kids, and they loved him. They all just seemed to need a little mothering. No wonder Emily had been so desperate about leaving Will in the lurch this summer. For the first time since she'd arrived, Erica was glad that she had come.

As they swung in companionable silence, the sun dipped low, behind the distant mountains, and one by one the stars appeared in the darkening sky. The wind whispered through the hazelnut leaves in the orchard, sending them dancing to the crickets' soulful tunes. Erica relished these sounds she never heard in the city. It was so peaceful sitting with Will on the porch swing that in a sudden fit of whimsy, she felt as if she could stay there, just like that, forever. Will must have felt it, too, for he turned to her and looked at her so strangely, she wondered if he could read her thoughts.

"Emily," he began, his voice gentle, his words tender. "I've never really thanked you for everything you've done for us since you started. I know it hasn't been easy for you—I pretty much disappeared when you arrived—and I'm sorry. Since June passed away, we've been through at least half a dozen of the most unbelievable nannies you'd ever want to meet. I'm really glad you came back, and I'm sorry that I left you to do all the work." His dark green eyes sparkled in the starlight as they found and locked with hers. "Sorry I never took the time to notice just what a wonderful woman you were before today."

Erica felt the warm pleasure of his words and the cold guilt of his innocent mistake meet in a riot of goose flesh on her arms. He was talking to the wrong woman.

Will shifted in his seat, and for one insane moment, Erica wondered what he would do if she planted a big fat kiss on those incredibly sexy lips. Ha. She was definitely losing it.

"Brother-in-law," she reminded herself, and then thought she'd faint when she realized she'd spoken the words out loud.

"Hmm?"

"Oh . . . nothing. I, ah, j-just remembered s-something," she stuttered.

"Oh." He grinned and took her slender hand in his. Squeezing it gently, he pulled this woman he'd known since May, yet not at all, slightly toward him on the swing.

"I just wanted to say . . . thanks. For coming back to the kids . . . ." His voice trailed off and he sat staring at her, tracing her knuckles with the rough pad of his thumb.

He seemed distinctly flustered. Nervously he wet his lips with the tip of his tongue, and tiny beads of sweat gathered on his upper lip. He was beginning to rub the skin off her knuckles, and Erica wondered once again if he was onto her little ruse.

Maybe she should throw him off track with that passionate kiss now, she thought wildly, and wanted to laugh at the absurd workings of her panicked mind. Why, oh, why, did she keep having these crazy thoughts about kissing this man? This was not like her at all! Perhaps it was because her sister had encouraged her to "dangle the bait." Well, her brain had sure taken that suggestion and run with it. If she ever acted on any of these little fantasies, Will would think she'd gone over the edge. And he'd be right.

Erica's mind raced as she considered the ramifications of a kiss. What if Emily eventually ended up married to Will? That would mean she'd played kissy-face with her brother-in-law! It was too awful to contemplate. No, no matter how curious she was about this man, he was strictly off-limits.

Patting her hand distractedly, Will finally managed to find his voice.

"Well, anyway, thanks." He focused his gaze on her lips and they sat for some time, sorting through a plethora of feelings, stymied as to what to do about them.

"Dad?" The screen door banged shut and Sam approached the porch swing, glancing suspiciously at her father and Emily sitting so closely together, holding hands. "The movie's over and we're going to bed. What are you doing out here in the dark?" she asked, fear creeping into her childlike voice.

"Just talking, sweetheart. We'll be in soon to tuck you in," Will told her, gripping Erica's hand in his. It was time his daughter got used to the idea that her father would someday get on with his life. And though it might be painful for her, it was the first healthy thing he'd done all year.

"Okay," she said uncertainly, backing up toward the door and turning quickly, before she bolted inside the house.

"She thinks something's going on between us," Erica murmured, feeling for the young girl.

"Would that be so bad?"

Erica shrugged helplessly, the weight of a thousand complex questions lying heavy on her heart. To get too deeply involved with Will and his kids could break her heart. To keep them at arm's length could break theirs. And going too far in either direction could break Emily's. *This is another fine mess you've gotten us into, Emily.*

"Well, how about that haircut?" Will stood and pulled her to her feet.

"Um-hmm. How about that haircut," she echoed. *Yes, Emily. Another fine mess.*

Chapter Three

"Cut it really short," Will instructed, dragging a wooden kitchen chair to the middle of the brightly lit room. The kids were tucked away for the night, and the two adults were alone. Neatly arranged on the countertop were the barbering tools Will had provided for her convenience.

Warily she eyed the scissors, comb and electric shears, and battled a burst of hysterical laughter. This was insane.

"As far as I'm concerned, you really can't cut off too much," he said blithely, and settled himself in his chair. "I like it really short in this heat. Besides, it grows pretty fast."

"Okey—" she sucked her breath in "—dokey." She blew it out. She stood behind Will and wondered where to start. The top? The back? The sides? Perhaps she should put a bowl on his head and chop off everything that stuck out. No, she'd never liked that look. Will sat waiting expectantly while she nervously pondered her first move.

"Something wrong?" he asked, and twisted in his chair so that he could see her face.

"Oh, no. No, nothing at all. Just—" she reached for the bath towel that lay on the counter "—trying to decide about the look I want to achieve. You can't rush these things," she added defensively.

Will shrugged. "Well, don't go getting too fancy. A simple haircut will do," he assured her, and turned back around.

"The simple look is the most difficult to achieve," she informed him, stalling for time. *Oh, please, Lord, let me do a good job.* Unfurling the bath towel with much ceremony, she draped it over Will's broad shoulders and tucked it securely around his neck. His shoulders were so strong. She couldn't resist lightly running her hands over their breadth.

"It's a little...tight," he gasped, struggling to loosen the noose she'd fashioned at his throat.

"Oh! Sorry!" she giggled. "I guess I must be used to...the kids' little necks," she improvised, and adjusted the towel to fit more comfortably. "Your neck is so...large."

A small smile played at his lips. It was? He guessed he'd never given it much thought.

Erica moved around the chair to stand in front of Will, and studied him thoughtfully. She reached for the comb and tapped it absently on the palm of her hand. Able to really look at him for the first time since they'd met, she was surprised at how handsome he was. Long, thick, sandy brown eyelashes tipped gold at the ends heavily framed a set of emerald green eyes that smoldered with latent sensuality. His rugged complexion glowed with the healthy bronze kiss of the summer sun. His upper lip curled slightly to one side, giving his strong, chiseled features a hint of boyish arrogance.

"I'm ready when you are," he told her expectantly.

The sound of his voice pulled her back to the task at hand.

"Let's get on with it, then," she said more to herself than to Will. She knew from her own experiences at the hairdresser's that she should probably comb through his hair first to make sure there were no tangles. Moving around behind him again, she tentatively touched the top of his head with her left hand. His hair was incredibly soft, she marveled, running her hand down its shaggy length. She would never have guessed it was this silky from looking at it. Gaining a bit of confidence, she began slowly combing through his fabulous mane. Seemed a shame to cut it at all it was so beautiful. Like spun gold, only darker, she mused, with little threads of silver here and there at his temples.

Pushing lightly on his forehead, she tilted his head back against her stomach and combed through the hair at the front of his head. He closed his eyes and groaned contentedly.

"Feels good," he murmured."

"Um-hmm," she agreed. *It felt incredible.* "I always like having my hair done at the salon," she said, nudging his head forward and combing the hair at the back of his neck. "There's just something about it. I don't know . . . it's just so much nicer than doing it myself."

"Umm."

As much as Erica wanted to stand there all night long, running the comb through Will's amazingly sexy hair, she knew she could no longer put off the inevitable. It was time to start cutting. Maybe she could just snip a little here and a little there and he'd be satisfied, she thought, picking up the large, unwieldy scissors.

"Short, now," he advised.

Maybe not.

Lifting a hand out from under the towel, he pointed at the electric clippers. "You can use those at the sides and back," he told her. "If you run them up from the neck, it leaves the hair about that long," he said, holding his fingers about a quarter of an inch apart.

Good Lord! He wasn't kidding. She'd have to cut off a good three inches to get his hair that short. Her heart shifted

into second gear. "Okay," she said, and took a deep breath.
Here goes nothing.

Erica combed a lock of his hair between her fingers and,
positioning the scissors, squeezed her eyes closed and cut.
A healthy inch of sandy brown hair floated down into his
lap, and Will picked it up, judging its length.

"No, shorter than that," he encouraged her, "Really, it's
okay."

Okay, buddy, you asked for it. She winced and set to
work, snipping and clipping, trimming and shaping, until
great golden brown piles of hair decorated his shoulders and
the floor. After a few minutes of practice, she gained momentum and began humming softly. This wasn't so hard,
she thought, relieved that she was finally getting the hang of
it. Maybe she'd go to beauty school, she mused, and give up
nursing altogether. This was kind of fun.

Trying to decide how close she was to being finished, she
walked around Will and surveyed her handiwork. Not bad!
Not half bad at all. Mentally congratulating herself, she at-
tacked the front of his head.

Straddling Will's legs, she balanced slightly above his lap,
the tip of her delicate pink tongue protruding, as she concentrated on her art. Her bust hovered at eye level, tantalizing him, and Will was greatly disconcerted to discover that
the moan he heard had come from himself.

"Are you all right?" Erica stopped chopping and tipped
his chin up to look at his face. "Did I cut you?" Concerned, she used the back of her wrist to brush the clip-
pings out of his eyes. When that didn't work, she blew
lightly on his face.

Clamping his teeth together, he bit back another groan of
frustration. *It's been way too long.* He flapped at the towel
with his hands, hoping against hope that it covered his lap.
"No, I'm fine. Stiff neck," he lied. Have mercy. He didn't
know how much more of this he could take.

"I'm almost done," she reassured him, and innocently once again offered her bust for his inspection. Snip, clip. Snip, clip. She arched her back and, leaning away from Will, ran her fingers through his hair and squinted.

Will's eyes dumbly followed the movements of her lithe body. Think of baseball, man, he commanded himself. First base, second base…third…base… Think of football, man.

"Hmm," she mused, running her tongue over her lower lip. "Blah!" Nose wrinkled and eyes crossed, she did it again. "Plaughck!"

"What?" Will asked in alarm. It couldn't look that bad.

"I got some of your hair in my mouth." She frowned, looking at her hair-covered hands in dismay.

"Here, let me see," he commanded, pulling on her wrist.

Sticking the tip of her tongue out at him, Erica forgot her inhibitions and complied. "Ith a tha end," she directed.

"Come closer, under the light." Will sat up straight for a better view. "Down. Lean back. Up." Try as he might, he couldn't see a thing. "Oh, for the love of… Come here," he said gruffly, and pulled her into his lap. Ignoring the warning voice that screamed *"Mistake"* in the back of his head, he angled her face in front of his and inspected her rosy pink tongue. "Oh, I see it," he said, and touched the warm, wet tip with his forefinger.

They froze, both of them fossilized with fear and wonder. Her lips involuntarily closed around his finger. Hearts hammering crazily, they sat and stared at each other, shocked at the feelings that coursed through their bodies.

Slowly Erica opened her mouth and released his finger. "I think you…got it," she said breathily, and mustering every ounce of strength she possessed, pushed off his lap to stand on shaky legs. "Thanks." She wobbled over to the counter, searching for a graceful escape from the amazing pull of Will's eyes.

"Sure," he answered, and squirmed in his chair. "Uh, there's an outlet behind the toaster." He pointed at the appliance in question.

What was he suggesting? Had she missed something here? He wanted a piece of toast? Now?

"For the clippers." He grinned at her confusion.

"Oh, yes, of course. For the clippers." Erica sprang to the toaster and pushed it aside. Plugging in the clippers, she strung the cord over to his chair and stared with great trepidation at this new wrench in the otherwise-smooth works. Her hands were shaking so badly she doubted she could turn the silly thing on, let alone use it.

"The switch is on the side," Will commented, noting the tremor in her hand.

"Oh." Erica somehow managed to turn the power on, and jumped as the clippers began to vibrate noisily.

Will nodded. "Just set the end against my neck and run it over the back of my head. It's easy."

Marshaling her powers of concentration, Erica did as she was told. And, much to her amazement, it worked. Slowly, with great precision, she evened out the ragged edges at the back and sides of his head, achieving a remarkably professional look. Short, but not too short. She had to admit that Will looked wonderful.

"Done!" she announced proudly, standing back to gaze at what her heretofore hidden talent had created.

"Great." Will beamed and ran his hands over his new do. "Feels good, too," he praised. "I don't suppose you could take a little more off the back, right here?" he asked, pointing to the back of his head.

"Where?" Erica stepped around to the back of his chair. "Oh, I see what you mean. Just a sec." Reaching for the clippers, she heard something clatter to the floor. Great, the stupid thing was falling apart just before she was finished. Must not be anything important, she thought, and turned the switch on. The clippers hummed to life, and she set them down on the area Will had pointed out.

That's funny. She blinked rapidly, trying to refocus her eyes on her work. It almost seemed as though she could... see...his...*scalp!* Jerking the clippers away from what was once his full head of hair, Erica stifled a scream. For there, shiny and pink as a newborn baby's bottom, lay a perfectly round, perfectly bald—spot.

Will had said short, but this? Good heavens almighty, what had she done?

"Uh, Will?" she squeaked, and turned off the clippers.

"What?" He could sense that something was amiss.

Erica cringed. "Remember when you said, 'Cut it really short'?"

"Yeah."

"Just exactly how short did you mean?"

"Why?"

"Oh, nothing..." Her voice had the tinny bleat of a frightened lamb. Good grief! How could she explain this? Maybe, she thought hysterically, maybe she could paint a little smiley face there and nobody would notice the difference. Talk about having eyes in the back of your head....

She'd done it now. Might as well tell the truth and wait for Will to throw her out on her ear. "Uh, Will?"

Will looked up at Erica's ashen face and suddenly knew for sure that something was wrong. Very wrong. "Are you feeling all right? You look sick."

The man had a talent for understatement. "Will, I think that, um, that something is wrong with the—" she licked her dry lips "—clippers."

"What?"

"Well, for some reason, they seem to have cut your hair shorter than usual just now," she explained lamely.

"How short?"

"Well," She closed her eyes and took a deep breath. "Short."

"Short like crewcut short?"

"No, actually more short like..." She cringed and took a step back. "Bald short?"

"What!" Shocked, Will reached up and awkwardly felt at the back of his head. Yep. She sure had that right. It was short like bald short.

Erica backed up to the kitchen table and slumped into the nearest chair, letting her head fall dismally into her arms. "Oh, Will," she babbled, past the huge mass that was forming in her throat. "I'm so sorry. I don't know what went wrong! It was so perfect and I..." She drew a ragged breath. *"Ruined it!"* she cried, all the tensions of her crazy day catching up with her at once. Unable to stem the flow of tears any longer, she dissolved into a puddle of wretchedness and sobbed as though her heart would break.

Will stood uncertainly and watched Erica's slender shoulders shake with emotion. She was taking this whole thing pretty hard. Actually, he thought, a slow smile spreading across his face, when you got right down to it, it was kind of funny. He bit back the laughter that welled in his throat. She didn't look as though she'd be able to appreciate the humor of the situation.

Taking a tentative step toward her, he heard a crunching sound come from beneath the sole of his boot. Uh-oh. The blade guard. The little piece of plastic that kept the clippers from cutting his hair too short. Oh, well. Erica's sobs grew more pathetic, and Will had to bite the inside of his cheek to keep from roaring with laughter. Bending down amid a flurry of shorn locks, he picked up the broken blade guard and tossed it into the sink. Maybe she could carve his name into the back of his head, he mused, the humor of this nutty situation gripping him. He could tell the kids he'd decided to go punk.

Reaching down, he stripped off his hair-covered T-shirt and brushed off his shoulders and chest with it. The harder

Erica cried, the more he wanted to laugh. She was really coming unglued.

"Emily," he began, and tried coughing to cover up a fit of hilarity. "It's, ha, hem…ha!" Will dragged his chair over next to hers and sat down. "Emily, please. Look at me," he said laughing and pushed her hair away from her tear-streaked face.

"I ca-ca-can't!" she wailed, and reaching up, covered her face with her hands.

"Oh, Emily." He chuckled, and patted her soothingly on the back. "Please, honey, stop crying. It will grow back. Honest." It had been a long time since Will had had to deal with a woman in tears, and curiously, something about the wilted woman flopped tragically across his kitchen table brought out his protective instincts. Good Lord, it wasn't the end of the world.

"Why, next week at this time, you won't even be able to tell at all." Gently he pried her hands away from her face and smiled at her. "Come on, now. Please, sweetheart. Please stop crying," he said, laughing, the ludicrous situation beginning to strike his funny bone all over again. Unable to hold back any longer, Will leaned back in his chair and roared with laughter. Oh, it felt good to laugh. He hadn't laughed this hard since…well, actually, he couldn't ever remember laughing hard enough to lose a major organ. Slapping his thighs with glee, he whooped loudly once more.

Slowly Emily opened her tear-filled eyes and peered with surprise at the half-naked man who sat a few short inches away from her, howling with delight at the ceiling. He was magnificent. She'd thought he had a good build, but nothing had prepared her for the washboard stomach, the well-formed pectorals, the bulging triceps, the smooth, broad, perfectly rounded shoulders. All of this and a sense of humor, too. No wonder Emily had such a crush on this man.

"You...you're not mad?" she asked, and wiped her nose with a paper napkin she'd plucked out of the holder on the table.

"Why should I be mad?" he gasped, and grabbed his own napkin to mop at his streaming eyes. "It wasn't your fault."

"It wasn't?" she sniffed, gazing at him doubtfully.

"Nnnn-no!" He wrapped his arms across his stomach to keep his sides from splitting wide open. Oh, this was getting painful. He rocked back and forth in his chair, fighting for air, and Erica began to feel better.

"If you don't count the, um, mistake, it looks pretty good," she said, and giggled. Picking a lock of his hair up off the floor she asked, "You have any superglue?"

Will howled.

Erica grinned sheepishly. "Maybe I should write to the Hair Club for Men about our problem," she said, beginning to laugh in earnest now. Will's laughter was infectious, and soon both of them were rocking with paroxysms of mirth.

For several moments they sat thigh slapping and screaming with hilarity their ideas for Will's new look. Finally, their laughter began to wane and they sat dabbing at their eyes and smiling at each other.

"I'm really sorry about—"

"Hey," Will interrupted, and reached out to grasp her hand in his. "Not another word. Honest, I'll only look like Friar Tuck for about a week. You'll never know the difference."

Oh, but I will, Erica thought, quickly glancing at his deeply tanned upper body. I will definitely know the difference. "Okay," she agreed shakily. "Thanks for being such a sport."

"Anytime. You know, it just dawned on me that I haven't laughed much in the past few years. It feels real good." He chuckled and squeezed her hand. "It's been a long, incredibly memorable day. We should probably go to bed."

Startled by the intimacy of his words, Erica was once again taken aback by the supercharged awareness that existed between the two of them. They both sat staring at each other, want and need reflected in their gazes, and wondered what to do next.

"I should probably..."

"Let's start..."

They laughed self-consciously.

"I was just going to say we should probably start cleaning up," Erica said, feeling bashful.

"Good idea." Will got up and went to the pantry for a broom and dustpan.

While he swept the floor, Erica wiped down the chairs and table, then put her hair-cutting tools in a tidy pile on the counter. When they were finished, Will snapped off the kitchen light, and suddenly the room was filled with darkness. The moon's soft glow filtered in through the window and it took her eyes a brief moment to adjust. Erica caught her breath as the pale light illuminated the powerful man she now worked for. He ran his hand across his chest and pulled open the door to the kitchen.

"Come on," he whispered, the lack of light making his hushed tone seem natural. "This way." As she reached him, he took her elbow loosely in his hand and led her through the shadowy house and up the stairs. They reached her bedroom door first and stood there, both uncertain how to go about ending the day. The old farmhouse creaked and groaned occasionally, as though settling in for the night. Other than the night sounds that sifted gently in through an open window at the end of the hall, all was quiet.

"I put your bags next to your closet," he informed her shyly. "Well, thank you again, for the haircut and all," Will whispered, giving her elbow a playful squeeze before dropping it. "Sleep tight, now."

She knew she probably wouldn't sleep a wink. "'Night," she answered, and disappeared into her room.

As she slipped between the crisp, cotton sheets, her last conscious thought was of Emily and her safety. They were both treading on dangerous territory, she mused. Hoping with all her heart that one, or both, of them would not end up hurt, she drifted off into an exhausted slumber.

The week that followed kept Erica so busy she had little time to worry about anything but her new family and trying to keep her facts straight. Remarkably, the Spencers took for granted that their nanny, although different in many respects, was still the same old Emily they'd known since May. Will had good-naturedly taken a lot of teasing about his hair from the kids, but true to his prediction, the bald spot had filled in quickly with stubble, leaving little trace of the unfortunate mishap with the clippers.

Much to Erica's relief, she was finally becoming accustomed to the children.

Danny was a sweet child, with the energy of a normal nine-year-old. He gave Erica few problems, other than driving his sister half out of her mind at times. Sam, on the other hand, was by fits and turns rebellious and friendly, depending on how quickly Erica met her demands.

But the person whose behavior baffled Erica the most by far was Will. Emily had promised Will would be out of the house by dawn, only to return for a few surly moments to eat. In reality, nothing could have been further from the truth. On most days Will would join her in the kitchen for a morning cup of coffee. Before he headed off to work, they would chat amiably about their plans for the day. Refusing to take a sack lunch with him to the orchard, he would return and have lunch with her and the kids. In the evening, again he would come into the kitchen after his shower, and keep her company while she prepared their dinner. After the evening meal, Will rarely spent time in the barn, but instead puttered around the house, whistling happily over his various projects.

Many times she could feel Will's eyes follow her through the routine she had established since she'd arrived, and wondered what he was thinking. Was he suspicious? And why on earth had Emily painted him as such an uncommunicative, silent type? Just how much attention did her incurably romantic sister need, anyway?

Erica was sure she was spending as much time in Will's company as most married couples spent together and she was beginning to worry about how she would keep Will at arm's length, yet entice him into Emily's boat at the same time. Not to mention the guilt she felt at being attracted to her sister's object of affection. And it didn't help matters one bit that ever since she'd cut his hair, he had been very playful with her. There were times Erica could have sworn that the gleam in Will's eye was more than just playful. More than just friendly. No, whether Will knew it or not, there were times that the possessiveness he was beginning to feel for his nanny was written all over his face.

This, of course, did not go unnoticed by Sam. Feeling her position as the leading lady in her father's life had been usurped, and finding Erica to blame, Sam was becoming more difficult with each passing day.

"Go ahead and eat." Erica nodded at the kids to start filling their plates. "We've waited long enough."

Sam exchanged a knowing glance with her brother.

"What?" Erica asked, looking back and forth between the two.

Sam drew herself up straight in her chair and affected her most grown-up pose. "He doesn't like it when we eat without him. He says it's the only way he gets to spend quality time with us," she informed Erica primly.

"Oh." Tough, she thought uncharitably. Will was over an hour late, and she was starving. "Obviously your father has some more work to do in the orchard, and I'm sure he won't mind if we make an exception this once."

"Okay..." Sam sang the word as if to say "It's your neck..." and dug into her salad.

"Danny?" Erica pulled a piece of garlic bread out of the foil.

"Whum?" he mumbled, and sucked a saucy strand of spaghetti into his mouth.

"Did you put your father's tools away?"

Danny's eyes grew suddenly wide.

Erica sighed. "Danny..." She shook her head in exasperation. "You promised me you would put them away."

With raised eyebrows and pursed lips, Sam said, "Boy, Dad's gonna be hot! He said we're *never* supposed to use his stuff!" She gloated as Danny fidgeted nervously in his chair. Turning to Erica with a haughty look, she informed her, "You shouldn't have let him use Dad's tools. He'll probably kill you," she stated grimly.

On account of a bunch of stupid tools? Erica smothered a smile at the girl's overly dramatic prediction. "Sam, that will be enough. Danny, as soon as you are done eating, I want you to go put those tools away."

Will was having a hell of a day. Everything that could possibly go wrong with his air-blast sprayer had gone wrong. Hot, sweaty and grumpy, he wanted nothing more than a cleansing shower and a cold drink. He would have had the stupid thing fixed and the whole damn orchard sprayed for filbert worm by now if he could just have found his blasted wrench set.

Tossing his toolbox in the back of his pickup, he decided to call it a day. He wiped his sweaty brow on the sleeve of his shirt and cursed the sprayer again. When a potent round of expletives didn't cure his temper, he ripped his Stetson off his head and smacked the sprayer fiercely, then kicked it a few times for good measure. Damn piece of junk. He pulled himself up into the cab of his truck and let his head thud against the rear window. Nothing could rid him of this foul mood. With the possible exception of the lovely Emily, waiting at home for him with a hot, delicious meal on the table, and his two adoring children, who sat eagerly waiting to tell him about their day.

From where she stood doing the dishes with Sam in the kitchen, Erica could hear Will yelling out in the barn.

"I told ya," Sam chortled as she scrubbed the spaghetti pot. "He's *really* sensitive about his tools. He's not going to be too happy about missing dinner, either."

Shooting the young girl a weary look, Erica blew at her bangs and sighed. "Sam . . ."

"What?"

The screen door banged shut and Danny ran through the kitchen, tears streaming down his cheeks. Picking up a dish towel, Erica dried her hands. "Finish up in here, will you?"

Sam opened her mouth to protest, then thought better of it. "Okay."

The wrench set in question lay strewn on the ground, just outside the barn's back door. Crouching on the ground, Will tossed the pieces into his toolbox and muttered various spicy bits of sage advice about showing some *damn* respect for people's personal property. At Erica's approach, he glanced up at her and scowled.

The black thundercloud over his head did not promote chitchat, so she decided to cut to the chase. "I heard what you said to Danny."

"Yeah." He tossed a wrench into the toolbox. "So?"

"So, don't you think you were a little rough on him?"

"Why don't you let me be the judge of that? It's *my* job to discipline the kids. They're *my* kids. I'll handle them."

Erica couldn't have been more stunned if he'd reached out and slapped her hard across the face. "I didn't say you shouldn't discipline them. I just said you were a little rough on him."

"Emily—" his tone was icy "—he lied to me about using the tools. He told me he hadn't touched them."

"Maybe he's afraid of you. Maybe that's why he asked me, instead."

Will gripped his knees and pushed himself to a standing position. He turned slowly to face her. "You should never have allowed him to use my tools," he spit, his eyes shooting green lightning. Erica could see the storm brewing behind those emerald eyes and shivered. He kicked his toolbox. "Do you have any idea how much time he cost me today?" A furious muscle twitched in his tightly clenched jaw.

"Just because you've had a bad day is no reason to ream the poor kid the way you did."

"And I think that perhaps you should butt out!" Will's voice rose angrily.

Erica closed her eyes against the pain of his words. She'd been wrong to become so involved with this family. Wrong for so many reasons. That was crystal clear now.

"By all means, Will." She sighed, tears of frustration and hurt pricking the backs of her eyelids. "Take care of *your* kids." She tossed this jab over her shoulder as she turned on her heel and angrily marched toward the dark shadows of the orchard to cool down. It was obvious he was in no mood to talk. And now, neither was she.

"Hey! Emily! Come back here!" he shouted after her.

"Kiss off," she muttered. Neck stiff and head high, she stalked away, till she was out of sight.

He could just go jump in the lake, she thought, her lower lip trembling uncontrollably. Darn it, anyway. Why was she crying? She didn't care what Will did with his kids.

Don't worry, June. Erica sent her vow heavenward and wiped her tears on the back of her hand. I won't let him get away with that kind of attitude. She would protect the kids. For June's sake, if nothing else.

Will stood staring after her, completely flabbergasted. What the hell had just happened here? He had thought he was coming home to a nice dinner with a beautiful woman. Ha. Instead he'd ended up with this debacle. Now everyone was mad at him. Including himself.

He waited for her to turn around and come back, and when she didn't, he pounded the side of the barn. Damn woman. She could just stew in her juices for a while.

"Kiss off," he snorted, and shook his head. "Huh... yeah, right."

Chapter Four

It had been over an hour, and still no sign of Emily. Will rocked slowly back and forth on the porch swing and contemplated going out to the orchard to find her. The kids were in bed and he'd had plenty of time to think about their fight. He knew that he'd overreacted. She was right. He should never have been so hard on Danny.

He swore softly under his breath and kicked the porch railing with the heel of his boot. *What a jerk!*

He was beginning to discover something out there in the warm summer twilight—something he hadn't known about himself until his argument with Emily. Will Spencer was beginning to discover that he was afraid. Afraid of losing his kids to Emily. Afraid of losing control over his children... losing control over his heart.

For some strange reason that Will couldn't exactly put a finger on, he found himself hopelessly attracted to Emily. She invaded his thoughts night and day, tantalizing him... teasing him.... Fighting with her had only been a feeble attempt to push her away. Something about Emily Brant

scared the hell out of him. And ever since the day she'd returned, over a week ago, there had been a tantalizing chemistry that neither of them could deny.

Will closed his eyes and let his chin rest in the palm of his
hand. He wasn't ready for this. He didn't want to need
anybody. He'd decided that, the day June and their baby
boy had died. Well—he blew the air out of his lungs in a
frustrated puff—it was too late now. He needed her—more
than he cared to admit. Hopefully she'd be pleased that he'd
apologized to Danny. Hopefully he hadn't blown it with her.
Yes. He needed her—and he needed her now.

Restlessly he stood and walked to the edge of the porch.
She'd been gone long enough, he decided, bounding down
the front steps and heading toward the orchard. Guided by
the light of a full summer moon, he strode through the
heavy foliage and thought back to a similar fight he'd had
with June about disciplining the kids. It seemed so long ago
now, he mused sadly. He could barely remember what all the
fuss had been about, but if memory served correctly, they'd
made up quickly and the whole thing had blown over. If he
was lucky, the same would be true for him and Emily. Emily. June would have liked the way she handled the kids, he
thought, a small, crooked smile playing at his mouth. There
was something very special about Emily.

Beginning to wonder if she'd gotten turned around and
perhaps lost in the shadows of his trees, Will increased his
pace. Tree limbs swished quietly at his passage, beckoning
him deeper into the orchard's shadowy depths. Dodging and
weaving, he moved quickly as he made his way through the
first of several large orchards on his property. Still no sign
of Emily. Where was she? he wondered, beginning to worry
in earnest now.

"Will?"

Erica's tentative voice came from behind a row of trees
just ahead.

"Yes, it's me," he answered softly, his knees suddenly weak with relief. She was safe.

Stepping directly into his path, Erica stood uncertainly and reached for a branch as if for support. Will continued toward her, until he could make out the shadowed contours of her face, nearly hidden in the gloaming.

"Are you all right?" he asked raggedly, wondering what he could say or do to make amends.

"I guess," she said, smoothing an errant wisp of hair away from her face with her hand. There were so many things she wanted to say she didn't know where to begin. She wanted desperately to tell him the truth. To apologize for lying about who she was, for interfering in his relationship with his son. She had to do it now, before she lost her nerve. "Will," she began, her voice thready with emotion. "Oh, Will, I'm so sorry...I..."

"Shh," he whispered, taking the final step that brought him so close he could read the sorrow in her eyes. He needed to connect with her, to make her understand how sorry he was, to let her know how much he appreciated what she was doing with Sam and Danny. Reaching out, he lightly grasped her arm and pulled her to him, and felt a shiver run through her body, even in this heat.

"Hey," he admonished softly, running his hand down her arm and taking her delicate hand in his, "don't. I was wrong. I should be the one to apologize. Honey," he said with a sigh, and tilted her face up to his, "I'm so sorry. I had no business saying those things to you. It's just that I had such a frustrating day." He slowly shook his head. "But, I know you're right. I should never take it out on the kids that way."

"Having a bad day now and then is understandable." She tried to ignore the intimacy of his touch as he reached up and pushed her hair back over her shoulder. His hand rested there as he toyed with a silky lock. He wasn't making this easy for her. She was anxious to get on with her confession.

Will continued before she could blurt out her true identity, throw herself down on the ground, arms around his ankles, and plead for mercy.

"I grounded Danny for a week." A muscle jumped in his jaw. "I can't abide lies. And definitely not from my family."

Erica cringed.

Laughing softly, Will said, "Don't worry, I was fair. And I made a few much-needed apologies of my own." He shrugged, struggling for the words to help her understand his behavior over the tool incident. "Maybe I'm a little jealous."

Now she was really confused. "Jealous?"

"You're so good with the kids. A natural. And they respect you. They've needed someone like you in their lives for a long time now. Sometimes I think you know their needs better than I do."

"But, Will..." Pulling her hair out of his hand, she tried to organize her jumbled thoughts. She couldn't think straight with him standing so close. "You don't understand. I'm not who you think I am at all...really, I'm..."

"I know that you're wonderful with my kids. I know that they need you." He pulled her into the loose circle of his arms and rested his cheek against her forehead. "I know that *I* need you," he said, his voice raw with the depth of his admission.

A sense of dizzying giddiness battled with the wave of guilt that settled like a rock in the pit of her stomach. *Will needed her.* And much to her delicious horror she realized she was beginning to need him, too. But what about Emily? Poor, homeless Emily. She, too, wanted this man and his children. It was all so terribly sad.

"No." The word came out in a strangled sob. "You can't mean me. You don't know what you're saying." She turned her head away from the comfort of his soft cheek and swiped at her tears.

Will pulled her against his chest, and gathered a handful of her hair in his hand, at the base of her neck. Tugging lightly on this satiny brown rope, he searched for and found her eyes. "Yes, sweetheart. I mean you," he said, and kissed the tip of her nose.

Drawing her with him, he leaned against the trunk of a tree and settled her firmly into the solid wall of his body. "I don't know what it is," he murmured, "but ever since you came back from that weekend in San Francisco, I can't seem to get you out of my mind. I don't understand it myself, but seeing you there, standing in front of the house, something just...clicked. It was like I was seeing you for the first time."

Erica stiffened.

He framed her face with his hands and rested his forehead against hers. "You felt it, too, didn't you?"

"Yes," she whispered, beginning to forget what she so desperately wanted to say.

"And—" he drew a ragged breath against her mouth "—you feel it now, don't you?"

"Yes."

Groaning, he settled his lips over hers with a sigh and let the ages of loneliness and pent-up frustration run their course. Like a man stumbling upon his magical oasis after years in the desert, he drank deeply from her sweet, exquisite mouth, trying desperately to quench his unending thirst. He drew strength from her, her warm body pulsing with life. When she slipped her arms around his waist and clung to him, eagerly returning his searching kiss, he thought he'd surely perish from the ecstasy.

The sultry summer night served only to fuel his heated desire, and soon the fires of longing and yearning were blazing to life, after lying dormant for so long. He needed to shed the last remnants of grief and pain, and bury himself in her vitality.

As if Erica could sense his quiet desperation, she yielded to him completely. Running her hands up his sides to his shoulders, she pulled herself up to her toes, struggling to draw closer still to a man who could never belong to her.

Perhaps she could have resisted her own need for him. The need that had been growing, against her will, since the day she'd arrived. But she couldn't resist his. Even though, somewhere in the deep recesses of her mind, she knew what she was doing was wrong. Hungrily she twisted against him, searching for a way to tell him with this kiss, to communicate with feelings, what it seemed there were no words to describe. Tearing her mouth from his, she kissed his neck, his strong jaw up under his ear, the delightful curl of his upper lip, with something akin to panic. He tasted of male, spicy and sweet, strong and powerful, like no man she'd ever known. She had to experience, if only this once, the thrill of Will's passion. What she was doing was strictly taboo, she knew, and yet she was powerless to do anything to stop it.

"Oh, Emily." Will's sigh was tortured as he caressed her fevered cheek. *"Emily."* Her name was a prayer, feather light on his lips.

Emily. Emily! Good heavens almighty, what was she doing? To Emily? To Will? To...herself. Emily. The word seared through her dazed consciousness like a bolt of white-hot lightning. Emily. Her twin. Her flesh and blood. Oh, what had she done? The guilt rose like a bitter bile in her throat, and Erica was suddenly afraid she'd be sick.

The change in Emily was immediately apparent to Will. He could feel her withdrawal, and though he didn't know her reason, he could understand her trepidation. He was feeling a bit blown away by the explosion they'd just shared himself. Emily was the first woman he'd kissed since June had died. The first woman he'd even felt like kissing, and the fact that he'd just passed some mortal milestone stunned him. He'd been so sure that these feelings—now flaring to life for his children's beautiful nanny—had been put to rest a long time ago with June.

"Will?" Erica shakily extricated herself from his embrace. Even though she knew he hated liars, even though her sister wanted her to carry out this charade, she had to let him know the truth, before it was too late. "Will, I have to tell—"

Will hushed her with a gentle finger across her parted lips. She sounded so vulnerable, and scared. Will understood perfectly. "Don't say anything. I know," he whispered as he pushed himself off the tree that had been supporting them. He knew that she was as afraid as he was of their overwhelming attraction. It was too soon to discuss it.

"Friends?" he asked. Shy hope tinged his question.

Because there was nothing else they could ever be, and because she was too sick at heart to resist, Erica nodded dumbly.

"Good," he murmured, and taking her hand in his, led her back to the house.

Erica prepared for bed that night numb with grief and guilt. The pain of her betrayal rested heavily on her heart as she crawled between the sheets and drew her body into a trembling fetal ball.

She had to find Emily as soon as possible, confess her sins and beg her sister's forgiveness. And then, hopefully—once she knew how dismally her scheme had failed—Emily would come back. She had to. For though Erica was beginning to feel deeply for Will and his kids, it was in all of their best interests that she quit. Leave Harvest Valley. Leave Will and the kids, never to return.

Expecting relief, a vindication of sorts, since she'd made the right decision, Erica was pained to discover that the agony was now only worse than ever. A single tear rolled down her cheek as she offered a prayer up to the star-filled heavens. *Please, please help me find Emily.*

The soft sigh of hazelnut leaves was the only response, that—and the twinkling wink of a distant star.

* * *

For three solid days, Erica attempted to find her sister, with no luck. Every day she would coax Will's old broken-down pickup truck into Harvest Valley on the pretext of stocking their kitchen with groceries and any other house-hold supplies she could drum up. Sneaking off to town by herself was easy, as Will and the children had an endless list of needs for the rapidly approaching camping trip.

Every day she would make fruitless calls from a phone booth outside the general store to every homeless shelter and refuge she could find in Los Angeles. And every day she would return home, loaded down with a truckful of sup-plies and the dwindling hope of ever locating Emily. Maybe she would be able to find her once they'd returned from their camping trip. In the meantime, all she could do was pray for her sister's safety, and her own sanity.

Erica had done her best to avoid Will and play it cool re-garding her growing feelings toward him, since that night in the orchard. But, despite her best efforts, she still found herself becoming hopelessly entangled in the Spencers' lives. They needed her, and it became increasingly clear with each passing day that she couldn't leave them. At least not until she could find her sister. And due to the guilt she carried because of a stolen kiss—a kiss she relived with vivid clar-ity no fewer than twenty times a day—she felt that she owed it to Emily to stay. To swallow her urge to run, and see this monstrous duplicity through to its end. Just as she'd prom-ised in another life.

Unfortunately for Erica, her aloofness was lost on Will. He was charming and witty, and as full of life as a school-boy in the throes of his first crush. Any excuse, it seemed, constituted a reason to touch her, wink at her, smile his lazy, off-kilter smirk at her. Unaware of the tumultuous burden she carried, Will was ardent in his powerful pursuit.

And to make matters worse, a bittersweet ache that came from growing attached to the children lodged permanently in the back of Erica's throat. Sam and Danny, oblivious to her pain, were fairly wriggling with anticipation over the prospect of leaving for the woods the next day. Their enthusiasm was so contagious, Erica found she was almost beginning to look forward to the three-day weekend herself. At least there would be other people around, to keep her from spending too much time alone with Will.

"No." Erica rolled her eyes at Sam's pleading expression.

"But *why?*" she squealed, stomping her foot in annoyance.

Will had decided to pack for the trip the day before they left, and unfortunately for Erica, Sam wanted to bring everything, including the kitchen sink. At the rate she was going, they would have to use a second vehicle, just for her clothes.

"Because we're only going to be gone for three days, that's why. You can live that long without your boom box. No one wants to hear that racket out in the woods, anyway." Erica knew if she had to listen to the Poison Death Bad Boys' greatest hits one more time, she would begin foaming at the mouth and run naked and screaming through the streets of Harvest Valley. "Furthermore, young lady, you can go unpack at least half the clothes you're bringing with you."

"But, *E-eh-ehm!* I *ne-e-ed* them! All of *the-eh-ehm!*" she whined, and jumped up and down dramatically, her arms crossed over her chest.

"What? You need a dress to go camping in? I think not. Come on, Sam. Give me a break."

"Give *me* a break, Em!"

"Sam." Erica's tone brooked no further argument. "All you're going to need is a swimsuit and a few pairs of shorts," she advised, dragging Sam's multitudinous luggage out of the trunk of Will's car.

Danny poked his head out from the interior of the car with a grin. "I didn't know they even made swimsuits in the petite buffalo size."

Erica took one look at Sam's quivering lip, and knew that Danny had struck a sensitive nerve.

"*I don't even want to go on this stupid trip!*" she shrieked, and ran bawling into the house.

"Way to go, Danny," Erica said, scowling at the sheepish boy. "For that inconsiderate and hurtful remark, you have the honor of carrying your sister's luggage back into the house."

"Aw, jeez, Em! Anything but that! I'm just a kid," he moaned, and fell out of the car, clutching at his throat.

"Just do it," Erica muttered, and went into the house to find Sam.

Erica tapped lightly on Sam's bedroom door.

"Go away" came the muffled order.

"Sam, honey, it's me, er, uh, Emily. May I come in?" Not waiting for her reply, Erica cracked open the young girl's door. She slipped inside, to find Samantha sprawled facedown across her bed, turned away from the door. Quietly closing the door behind her, she crossed the room and perched awkwardly at the edge of the child's twin bed.

Taking a deep breath, Erica opened her mouth to express words of comfort that would not come. She closed her mouth and frowned. What did one say to a plump, hurting thirteen-year-old girl? Emily hadn't given her the recipe for success with this particular circumstance. She guessed she'd just have to wing it. Closing her eyes tightly, she tried to remember how it felt to be thirteen. Hmm, not pretty. But at least she'd had Emily and her mother to share her pain with. Sam didn't have a woman to confide in. Well, seeing as she was the only woman in Sam's life at the moment, she'd take a stab at it.

Reaching across the bed to the sniffling girl, she smoothed her tangle of ebony curls away from her porcelain cheeks. Sam would be a raving beauty in the not too far future. She hoped Will was up to coping with that. The idea of Will chasing Sam's suitors back down his long driveway brought a tender smile to her lips. She'd love to be here for that.

"Do you want to talk about it, honey?" Erica murmured, and when Sam shrugged disconsolately, she forged blindly ahead. "You know, I was thirteen once."

Sam opened one red, swollen eye and looked back over her shoulder at Erica. "Were you fat, too?"

Something about the hopeful, childlike quaver in the young girl's voice brought forth a burst of maternal instinct in Erica. She laughed. "Well, no. I had another problem."

Sam rolled over on her back and looked at Erica curiously.

"I had to wear braces on my teeth. And if that wasn't bad enough, for a while I had to wear some pretty awful head gear." She smiled at the memory. "It looked like I had on a UHF TV antenna around my head."

Sam's giggle was watery. "Your teeth were that bad?"

"Terrible. They went north, south, east and west. Every direction but down. I could have eaten corn on the cob through a picket fence." That wasn't exactly true, but Erica loved the smile it brought to Sam's face. "It's tough being thirteen. I know. But, Samantha Spencer, I can honestly tell you that you are one of the prettiest girls I've ever seen."

Sam blushed at the unfamiliar praise. "One of the porkiest, you mean."

"Oh, I don't think so. Anyway, I think you look like you've lost some weight," she said, and leaning back, critically eyed Sam's waistline.

Sam brightened. "You think so?"

"I sure do." It was true. Sam was definitely looking slimmer. "You're probably beginning to stretch out a little."

"I bet it's all that broccoli you make us eat."

"That too."

"People say I resemble my mom." She smiled at Erica. "My mom was really pretty," she said proudly.

Erica thought about the pictures she'd seen of June downstairs in the living room and nodded seriously. "She was a beautiful woman. And it's true. When you're all grown up, you'll look a lot like her."

"Do you really think so?" she asked bashfully. Casting her dark, heavily fringed lashes downward, she plucked at the threads of her chenille bedspread. "I miss her. It's hard to talk to my dad about some stuff."

Nodding sympathetically, Erica asked, "What stuff?"

"Girl stuff," she mumbled. Her ivory cheeks were suddenly stained with two bright patches of crimson.

Erica fidgeted uncomfortably. Good heavens. She didn't have to tell the child about the birds and the bees, did she? Where did one start? She had a hard-enough time saying certain body parts aloud, let alone describing their function to a child. Silently cursing Emily, she croaked, "Girl stuff?"

"You know..."

Erica nodded blankly.

"Like bras and stuff." Sam looked as though she wanted to jump out the window.

Ah, now bras... that Erica could talk about. Her eyes strayed involuntarily down to Sam's questionable bust and back up to the mortified teen's face. It didn't really seem that Sam needed a bra at this point in time, but then again, needing and wanting were two different things.

"How would you like to go bra shopping with me?" Erica asked, attempting to seem offhand.

"When?" Sam asked eagerly.

"Well, when we get back maybe?" At Sam's crestfallen expression she added, "Or this afternoon after you've unpacked a bunch of your clothes."

Sam sat up and threw her arms around Erica. "Thanks, Emily." She sighed.

Erica smiled and hugged her tightly in return. "You're welcome, sweetheart."

"Where are the kids?" Will asked, stepping between the back of the car and the travel trailer.

"In the house. I gave them a list of food and supplies to set out on the kitchen table," Erica responded absently, watching him. Muscles straining, he lifted the trailer off the ground.

"Umm," he grunted. "That oughta keep 'em busy for a while," he said through his tightly clenched jaw as he pulled the unwieldy contraption forward, toward the bumper.

Unable to help herself, Erica stepped closer to get a better look. She tried to ignore the stab of attraction she felt as she watched him perform these masculine duties. "Can I give you a hand or something?" she asked, marveling at his strength.

Groaning, he settled the trailer onto the car's hitch. "Nope." He exhaled mightily and smiled at her. "I got it." He dusted his hands off on the seat of his blue jeans. Turning on his heel, he strode toward the barn, motioning for her to join him.

"Come on. You can help me get the tents out of the loft."

Erica followed Will into the cool and shadowed interior of the dusty old barn. It smelled of hay and rope, motor oil and machinery, among other mysterious wonders that make up the magic of farm life. Crunching across the creaky pine floor, she mounted the steep staircase behind Will and pulled herself up into the hayloft. It was stuffy and hot, and nearly too dark to see. Will pushed open the hay door and it swung wide, banging loudly against the exterior wall of the barn.

"Over here." He motioned with his head and crossed over to a large, tarp-covered mound resting against the wall. "I keep the camping gear covered. It's dusty up here," he added unnecessarily. Dust fell like snowflakes from an invisible cloud in the bright sunlight that flooded in through the open door.

"What was Sam so fired up about?" he asked, grinning crookedly as he concentrated on his task.

"Danny said something that hurt her feelings." Erica wandered over to the opposite end of the tarp. "I had a talk with her and I think she feels a little better now." They'd had a silent understanding ever since the night of their fight. Erica was an equal partner in discipline and they would back each other up without question.

Bending down, she started untying one of the knots. "Uh, Will," she began, glad that she had something to occupy her hands.

"Hmm?" His brow was furrowed as tightly as the knot he was working on.

Taking a breath, she stoically blurted, "Sam wants a bra."

"What for?" His brow knitted tighter still.

"To use as a slingshot on Danny," she groused, exasperated with the obtuse male mind. She didn't want to have to explain "girl stuff" to him.

Will's eyes darted up to hers in surprise.

"I'm going to take her in to town to get one when we're through here," she announced, wrestling with her knot.

"I've got an old slingshot she can have," he offered, perplexed.

"Oh, Will." Erica burst out laughing. "She wants to *wear* it."

"A slingshot?"

"No!" she giggled. "A bra!"

"Why?"

"Because it's time. Will, she's thirteen. And..." She smiled softly at Will's fierce paternal expression. "She's growing up."

"Aw, jeez," he muttered, and rocked back on his heels, letting his hands dangle between his legs. "Already?"

Erica nodded.

He reached up and rubbed a throbbing muscle in his shoulder. "I'm terrible at that sort of thing."

"Most dads are." She shrugged lightly. "Uh, I don't suppose you've told her about..." She felt her cheeks grow hot.

Will's upper lip curled slowly. "Didn't have to. June took care of that years ago." He set back to work on the knots, and they worked together in the muted silence of the old hayloft for a moment, moving slowly toward the center of the tarp.

"Thanks," he said with a sigh when they met in the middle.

Erica slipped the last tie through the rivet. "Oh, sure."

"I mean for handling the... bra thing," he said, his windpipe constricting painfully. Kneeling beside her on the floor, his eyes strayed to hers, and he looked suddenly lost. "It won't be long till she's all grown-up, with a life of her own."

And he would be alone. Erica read the subtext of his plaintive words, and her heart ached for him. She reached over and gave his solid arm a reassuring squeeze. It must be especially hard for Will, to watch his children growing up, without his wife. Each milestone they passed signified yet another step away from the nest.

They gazed at each other helplessly, powerless to stop time and live forever in this perfect moment. Slowly Will helped her to her feet. They stood transfixed, sharing the bittersweet knowledge that time marched heartlessly on. His eyes caught and held hers, his face betraying his need for another clock-stopping kiss.

She was a woman torn. Erica valiantly battled the compulsions that inevitably drew her into the the haven of Will's embrace. She stood, unspeakably tempted, tenaciously clinging to the last shred of her diminishing control. It couldn't be happening again. She'd promised herself it wouldn't. At his frustrated sigh, she lost her grip and tumbled heart first over the edge.

Will pulled her roughly into his arms, and it seemed the most natural thing in the world to offer her lips up to his. All reason abandoned her, and she lost herself in the sweetness of the moment, lifting her arms, twining them around his neck. She whispered his name, a ragged plea of sorts, asking him to give what didn't belong to her.

How had this happened? She loved him and he belonged to Emily. He was Emily's, and Lord help her, she loved him. When it had happened, the precise moment she began to love Will, she couldn't say. Love at first sight was something the whimsical Emily believed in, not sensible, level-headed Erica. But here she was, less than two weeks into her job, in love with her sister's man.

He backed her up against the wall, his mouth never leaving hers, and leaned heavily against her body. She reveled in their glorious kiss with a passion that stunned her. His mouth moved roughly over hers, stealing her breath, leaving her weak with his urgency. This was where she belonged, she realized hazily, mindless beneath his powerful onslaught. Desperately Erica surrendered to the waves of pleasure, and returned his potent kiss, exulting in his response.

His mouth, it seemed, was born to fit hers, and she greedily claimed it for her own, heedless of the price she knew she would pay in guilt. Clinging to him for all she was worth, she sought to ease the ache of his emptiness...of her betrayal.

Outside, she could vaguely hear Sam and Danny arguing angrily, the voices growing louder as the children came toward the barn. Will dragged his mouth from hers and, breathing heavily, leaned his forehead against hers.

"How long until they find us?" he whispered against her lips.

"I don't know, but we'd better stop," she breathed, nuzzling his neck and his cheeks. "I don't think Sam could handle this." She was having a hard time with it herself.

"No," Will agreed, drawing her earlobe into his mouth, nibbling it, teasing it with his teeth. "We'd better stop," he muttered, and took her mouth again with a passion that was nowhere near ending.

"I'm gonna tell!" Danny's voice came from below them, inside the barn. "Daaaad!"

"Shut up, you little zipper head," Sam groused, clomping in after him.

Will's smile was rueful. "Time's up," he said, and kissed her hard, one last time. He ran a gentle hand over her hair, straightening it, then her collar. He stroked the roses in her cheeks left by the abrasion of his whiskers.

"So it would seem," Erica said blankly, still stunned by the myriad of dark and forbidden feelings that left her both thrilled and chilled.

The children clambered into the hayloft, and as they noisily vied for their father's attention, her eyes glazed over and she retreated into her silent world of shame.

Watching Will ruffle Sam's dark hair, she knew that because of what she'd just let happen, she would eventually lose them all.

Chapter Five

"They're asleep already," Erica whispered, and twisted back around to settle into the front passenger seat.

Will angled the rearview mirror to check on his children, then adjusted it back into position. "They're kind of angelic when they're zonked out like that," he said with a chuckle, keeping his voice low so that he wouldn't disturb them.

"Um-hmm," Erica agreed, enjoying the peaceful hush of the car's interior. Sam and Danny, excited as they were, had literally passed out before they'd reached the end of Will's long driveway. It was still a little too early for them.

Wispy clouds glowed pink on the horizon, promising a majestic sunrise at any moment. It was so cozy there in the car with her new family, the kids asleep in the back, Dad at the wheel and Mom...well, Mom was a fraud. But that did not mar the harmonious, nearly otherworldly peace that settled over Erica as she sat next to Will.

She'd tossed and turned most of the night, agonizing over what to do about this unbearable situation. Tortured by shame and worry over her growing attraction to Will, she'd thrown back the covers and padded over to her bedroom window, where she perched on the sill and gazed sorrowfully at the twinkling stars.

And it was then that a most amazing thing happened. From somewhere in the vast star-filled heavens came an overwhelming sense of calm acceptance. She was beginning to see that there was nothing she could do about this mess. Nothing. It would run its natural course, whether she liked it or not. And having finally come to that realization, she knew she could spend the next month wallowing in misery, or she could change her attitude and enjoy what little time she had left with Danny and Sam. And . . . Will. Feeling ten pounds lighter, she crawled back into bed and fell into the first peaceful slumber she'd had since she'd arrived.

The next morning, she'd jumped out of bed, a song on her lips, as excited as the kids to get this show on the road. She would allow herself to go away with this family, forget about the rest of the world and throw herself wholeheartedly into her job. That's what she was getting paid to do. That's what Emily wanted her to do. That's what the Spencers wanted her to do. Who was she to fight city hall? So, Erica chose to ignore the little voice in the back of her conscience that warned her not to get too attached. The voice that warned her to stay away from Will. The voice that warned her not to hurt her sister. No, she was simply there to have a good time, just like everybody else.

Will had insisted on leaving at the crack of dawn in order to make the two-hour car trip to pick up the kids' aunt July and uncle Charlie and their family in St. John's. From there, they would all drive for another couple of hours, to Ruby River, where they would raft all afternoon to the first campsite.

"Coffee?" Erica held up the thermos she'd packed.

"Sounds good." Will smiled. "Looks like you thought of everything."

"I hope so." She frowned. "Did we turn off the stove?"

"Yes." Will's low chuckle was warm. "Try to relax. This is going to be fun. Tell me about your shopping trip with Sam yesterday afternoon," he suggested, changing the subject.

Erica handed him a steaming cup of hot coffee and glanced back at Sam to make sure she was still asleep. She smiled fondly at the young girl, her riot of raven curls falling into her closed eyes, her lips parted softly in repose.

"Oh, Will," she whispered, a smile twitching at her mouth. "You should have been there. It was so cute."

"No, thanks." He grinned over at her, eyes twinkling. "I don't know the first thing about shopping for...women's underwear. What happened?" he asked, taking a sip of his coffee as he pulled onto the main highway to St. John's.

"Well, when we got to the mall, Sam was suddenly shy. She wanted me to run in and grab a bra for her while she hid on the floor of the truck. I practically had to drag her into the store." Erica poured herself a cup of coffee and tucked the thermos under the front seat.

"When we finally got into the store, this giant grandmotherly woman pounced on her and asked if she could help. Oh, Will, I've never seen anybody turn that shade of red," Erica giggled.

Will looked over at her and grinned. She was so pretty, he thought, watching her bring her coffee up to her mouth. That soft, warm mouth he couldn't seem to get out of his mind. "Then what?"

"Sam whispered, 'I want a bra.' Of course the old lady can barely hear and she yells, 'What, honey? Speak up, I can't hear ya!' I'm not kidding, Will, everyone in the entire store was staring at us. I just know Sam wanted to die." Erica glanced back at Sam, her face filled with maternal pride. "So, Sam managed to squeak, 'I want a bra,' and the saleslady booms, 'A bra? You sure?' Oh, Will, it was so awful!"

Will tried to hide his mirth behind a sympathetic smile. Biting the inside of his cheek, he said, "Must be tough."

"For a minute, I thought Sam was going to faint. The old sales gal grabs her and hauls her over to the bra department, where she makes this huge production over measuring Sam, right out there in the middle of the store. All the while, she's jabbering at the top of her voice, about cup size and support. Every time she used the word *bosom*, Sam would cringe."

A gleeful laugh escaped Will's tightly clamped lips.

"Hush, now," Erica scolded teasingly, and continued to whisper. "So, she rounds up an armload of bras and our Sam, poor thing, and herds her to a dressing room."

Pausing, Erica took another swig of coffee. Will couldn't help but notice how she'd called his daughter 'our Sam.' The joy he felt at those two simple words amazed him.

"The dressing-room door faced out into the store, Will! And I'm not kidding here, she actually gave a *demonstration* on how to wear a bra."

With a grin, Erica set her coffee cup down on the dashboard and demonstrated for Will. "She tells Sam, in her very loud, very shaky—you know, like an opera singer—old voice, 'Once you have it on thusly, you must bend allll the way over and let the boozums fall into the cups!' Then shake—" Erica wiggled wildly "—and hook...and...up!" She sprang back up in the seat, and they laughed as loudly as they dared.

"Poor Sam!" Will said, looking genuinely sorry for his daughter's trauma.

"Shh, quiet." She turned to check on Sam and Danny. Still asleep. Good. "But wait," Erica told him. "There's more."

"More?" Will asked incredulously.

"Oh, yes. The old gal kept yanking open the dressing-room door to see how Sam was coming along. She wouldn't even warn her. And," Erica gasped, "to make matters worse, Sam spotted a boy from her class. One of the cool ones, apparently."

"Oh, no."

"Oh, yes! She looked so helpless, Will. When the old battle-ax tottered off for another load of brassieres, Sam grabbed me and locked me in the dressing room with her and swore she was never coming out again."

"Finally, the boy left. Sam grabbed the first bra at the top of the pile and shoved it into my hands, before running out of the store as though the hounds of hell were after her. I couldn't find her at first . . . I thought maybe she'd walked home. But there she was, out in the main part of the mall, hiding behind some plants."

Still laughing over the story, Will handed her his empty coffee cup. She loved his laugh, so deep and warm it vibrated throughout her body. He looked so young when he laughed, all the stresses of his job and the kids ebbed away, leaving him relaxed and happy. Erica could tell by the appreciation in his eyes that he loved being with her, laughing with her, sharing a sense of humor that only the two of them seemed to spark together. She knew she had never laughed this much or this hard with anyone else. She hoped it was the same for him.

"It sounds like you had quite the day." His voice was filled with gratitude. There was no way he could have handled that situation with as much grace and aplomb as she had, and he would be forever grateful. "Thanks," he whispered.

"Oh, sure. Thankfully it's over now and Sam has her bra. On the way home, she was quite chatty. . . ."

Something in Erica's voice piqued Will's curiosity. "What'd she have to say?"

"A lot of things, really." Erica thought back to the girl's revealing comments. "But . . ."

"But what?"

"Well, she made it pretty clear that you won't ever need to remarry, because she can take care of you now. Especially, now that she's... a woman."

Erica saw the look of pain cross Will's handsome face; his jaw twitched with conflicting emotions. She knew how much his heart ached for Sam, growing up without a mother. Squeezing his arm lightly, she said, "Don't take it so hard, Will. She's okay. We had a talk. I think she's beginning to understand that someday she will want to move away, and that you will want to get on with your life."

Will shrugged and smiled helplessly at this wonderful, understanding woman, who had so fortunately come into their lives. "Thanks," he murmured, smiling ruefully at her. "You've been so great with her. I don't know how I can thank you enough."

Erica glowed warmly under his praise. "It's no big deal."

"Yes, it is. You have no idea what we went through with some of the nannies before you came along."

"Really?" Erica asked, curious about her predecessors.

"Umm..." Will nodded, passing a slow-moving vehicle. The sun was up now, bathing the car's interior with its warm rays. And though the scenic countryside was stunning in its beauty, Erica was much more interested in the man at her side.

"What were they like?" she asked, wondering somewhat jealously if any of them had been young and beautiful.

"The first one, Mrs. Tevit, spent more time charting our astrological signs than looking after the kids. She wouldn't make a move without consulting her crystal ball. Danny swears he caught her trying to ride the broom. She claimed she was sweeping the porch, but, you know kids and their imaginations. Her last day was the day she threatened to contact June and tell her how naughty they were being. Both of 'em had nightmares for days," he said grimly.

"How awful!" Erica was horrified. "How many nannies have you had?" She urged him to continue.

"A bunch, but she was one of the more colorful ones. And then there was Mrs. Ritner, ex-army. Military corners on the beds, mess hall-style grub and—" Will laughed and winked at Erica "—a tiny mustache, just like Hitler."

"Aughhh!" Erica giggled.

"I never had an urge to kiss her," he whispered. His eyes darted to her mouth and lingered for a moment.

Erica's cheeks grew warm under his scrutiny, and for lack of something better to do, she turned and checked on the kids. Looking at their sleeping faces, she was suddenly so very glad she was still there for them. She might not be the world's best nanny, and maybe she was pretending to be someone else, but she cared deeply for all three of them, and that was the plain and simple truth. She couldn't leave them now, even if she wanted to, and amazingly enough, she didn't want to.

Before she could stop herself, and much to her chagrin, she found herself asking, "How many of your nannies have you kissed?" Erica blushed as pink as Sam in the dressing room.

His expression was playful. "None," he said, flexing his hands on the steering wheel. "Never occurred to me. In fact, I never even thought about kissing you, till that day you came back from San Francisco," he admitted.

"Really?" She had to know the truth. Had to know that it was her, and not Emily, Will was kissing. Why that should make any difference was not clear to Erica, but it did.

"Really." He glanced over at her, his upper lip curling into that Elvis-style smirk of his. "I was kind of scared. I mean, all those weeks we barely spoke and then—"

One of the kids began to stir in the back seat. "Are we there yet?" Danny asked sleepily. Yawning and stretching, he pulled himself forward and poked his head between Erica and his dad.

"Just around the next corner." Will winked at Erica again. "Just around the next corner."

"You always say that," Danny complained, and flopped back in his seat, rudely awakening his sister.

Their peaceful solitude was over, Erica mused sadly. Just when she was beginning to sort out some of what was happening between her and Will.

"Danny, stop it!" Sam whined, and shoved her brother's feet over to his side of the car.

"Dad, Sam's shoving!"

"Well, he's kicking me!"

"Am not."

"Are, too!"

Will turned around and glared at the kids. "If I have to pull this car over—"

"Will! *Look out!*" Erica shrieked as he drifted into the oncoming lane of traffic.

Whipping back around in his seat, Will jerked the car out of the path of the RV that bore down on them, and sighed with relief. "Thanks," he muttered.

Danny pinched the front of his shirt at his chest and stretched it out dramatically. "Sam thinks she's big now that she has boobs! Auggh!" he yelled when Samantha punched him in the chest.

"You're the only boob in this car!" she cried.

Will and Erica exchanged soulful glances. Oh, for the peace and quiet of the wee morning hours.

"Who wants a sandwich?" Erica asked brightly, hoping to distract the squabbling faction in the back seat.

"I do, but first I have to go to the bathroom reeeeally bad!" Danny wriggled uncomfortably.

Will sighed. "Hang on, kiddo, there's a rest area coming up."

They arrived in St. John's at about bottle fifty of the second time through the "beer on the wall" song. As they rounded the corner of the street where the Martins lived, Sam and Danny began to bounce in the back seat and point excitedly at their cousins' house. Both of them craned their necks between Will and Erica for a better look.

"There it is!" Sam shouted. "And look! What's the matter with Uncle Charlie?"

As they pulled into the Martins' driveway, Erica could see the uncle in question, rolling around on the front lawn, in obvious pain.

"That's Uncle Charlie for you," Danny informed her knowingly. "He's always falling down or crashing into something. Dad calls him Uncle Clumsy."

"Danny...ahem. That will be enough," Will ordered, trying not to laugh as he pulled to a stop.

Unable to deny her years of nursing, Erica hopped out of the car and rushed to Charlie's aid.

"What happened?" she asked gently, kneeling next to Charlie's prone form.

Her voice was all business, Will noted, as he joined her on the ground. "Hey, Charlie," he joked nervously. "Lying down on the job?"

"Nah." Charlie attempted to laugh and grinned sheepishly. "Just conked myself in the head with that blasted tent pole there." He pointed at a long, heavy metal pole lying on the lawn next to him. "Hi, I'm Charlie Martin," he said woozily, and held a polite hand out to Erica. "You must be Emily. Glad to know you."

Charlie reminded Erica vaguely of the absentminded professor. Awkward and gangly, he was handsome in an almost goofy, boyish way. She instantly liked his kind, albeit battered, face.

"I'm happy to meet you, too. Looks like you broke your glasses." She held the shattered horn-rimmed glasses up to the light. "Hold still now," she ordered, and when she had finished taking his pulse, she checked his eyes and probed his head lightly with her fingers. "No concussion," she announced, "but you'll probably have a humdinger of a headache. Got any ice?"

He nodded. "In the house. July always keeps an ice pack ready for me," he admitted, clearly embarrassed to meet her under such ignominious circumstances.

Erica stood. "I'll get it—you stay put," she commanded, and headed for the house.

Will stared at her retreating back in surprise. Since when was she so proficient in first aid? Why hadn't she become queasy at the sight of the huge bump on Charlie's head? A week after she'd started working for him, Danny had gotten a nasty cut, and Emily had taken one look at all the blood and nearly fainted dead away. He was still puzzling over this when Erica returned with the ice pack. A flustered and excited July appeared right behind her.

"Oh, Charlie!" she admonished. "Honey! Really!" July was an older version of her niece, Sam. Dark, curly hair, lily white alabaster complexion and blue-gray eyes so translucent a person would swear she could see into her soul. She fluttered to Charlie's side with the ice pack and stroked his ruler-straight hair out of his face. "Poor baby," she murmured, and kissed the cleft in his chin, earning a loving smile from her man.

The four Martin children came charging out of the house, having heard the commotion in the front yard. Squealing with delight, they ran to their cousins and frolicked around their prostrate father.

Apparently they were used to seeing him like this, Erica mused, as July helped her still-dazed husband to his feet.

"I'm okay, honey," Charlie reassured her, and patted her tenderly on the back. "Go on inside with Emily," he suggested. "Will and I can finish loading the van." He pulled his polyester pants up high on his waist, revealing droopy black socks and a pair of battered saddle shoes. Pounding Will manfully on the back, he wiped his nose on his shirt sleeve and strode bowlegged toward the garage. "Come on, Will, old boy," he called, and disappeared through the door.

Satisfied that Charlie would live, July smiled warmly at Erica and invited her into the house. Erica waved at Will and nervously followed his sister-in-law. She might as well start making good friends with this woman now, she reflected, as she would probably end up being one of Will's sisters-in-law someday, too.

"You remember the kids, don't you?" July asked conversationally. Much to Erica's extreme relief, she pointed out each one of her children and repeated their names. "My eldest daughter, Rachel, is Sam's age. Travis is a year younger than Danny. Hannah, over there with Noah is seven, and he is four." She lead Erica into the large, airy kitchen and poured two cups of coffee. "You still like sugar and cream?" she asked, carrying the cups to the kitchen table.

This was so strange. Emily liked the works in her coffee, not Erica. "Uh, no, black is fine," She took her cup from July. "I'm trying to cut down on all that fat and sugar."

"Ah." July nodded. "Seems to be working on Sam. She's looking slimmer."

Erica glanced out the window into the front yard and smiled at her two kids. "Yes, she's lost several pounds in the past few weeks."

July studied Erica thoughtfully. "How long has it been since I saw you?"

Erica was at a complete and total loss. Will had mentioned that July had come to get the kids for a day that summer, but she had no idea when, or what they had talked about. "It seems like forever," she ventured, and shook her head, hoping July didn't catch the nervous twitch at the corner of her mouth. July's blue-gray eyes pondered at her so intently, Erica was beginning to wonder if she'd figured out that she was not Emily.

"Mom." Hannah skipped into the kitchen, her cheeks flushed from playing outside.

"What, honey?" July reached out and pulled her daughter to her side.

"What are woozums?" Large, curious blue eyes looked to July for the answer to this mysterious issue that Sam and her big sister had been giggling over.

"Woozums?" July gazed quizzically at Erica.

"Hannah." Erica grinned at the toothless child. "Do you mean bosoms?"

"Yes!" Hannah nodded and frowned. "What are they?" She glanced back and forth between the two women, both of whom were struggling to keep a serious face.

"Uh, Mom? Do you want to field this one?" Erica asked.

"Sure." July wiggled her eyebrows at Erica. "Honey," she said earnestly, "if I give you a box of Popsicles, would you give them to your cousins and brothers and sister?"

"Yeah!" Hannah jumped for joy, the "woozum" issue forgotten.

"Very smooth," Erica complimented her.

"Yeah, well, you'll learn. I see you're already helping Sam grow up. I'm so glad." July sighed sadly. "She needs a woman in her life." She went to the freezer, handed her daughter the promised Popsicles and rejoined Erica at the table.

Erica didn't quite know what to say. June had been July's sister, and for some reason, she almost felt as though she were trespassing on sacred territory. Although if July thought so, too, she gave no sign. She was so warm and easy to talk to, Erica found herself suddenly confiding in her.

"We've had our ups and downs. Sam isn't always wild about some of the decisions I make. I get the feeling she isn't always wild about me, either."

"What?" July refilled their cups. "Of course she is. She said lots of wonderful things about you last month or whenever it was."

Last month. Last month she'd been Emily. Sam loved Emily. For some reason, Erica felt strangely depressed.

July followed Erica's gaze out the window, where the men were loading the last of the Martin camping gear into Will's travel trailer. "I'd like to see Will marry again," July mused distractedly. "He needs a woman in his life, too."

She darted a glance at Erica, who appeared to be in some kind of trance she was so deep in thought. Erica didn't respond. July didn't seem to require one.

It was cool in the air-conditioned kitchen, but it must have been getting hot outside, for Will reached down and stripped off his T-shirt, then continued to load the vehicles. Erica sat and compared the two men—Charlie in his nerdy dad garb, and Will in nothing but a fabulous tan and an old, faded pair of jeans. Next to Will, Charlie looked even more pathetic than he would have on his own, Erica was sure. She admired the way Will's body moved, smooth and graceful, like an animal in the wilds. Muscles flowed and rippled under his firm brown skin. He was beautiful.

Erica knew that beauty was a lot more than skin-deep. But she had to wonder what exactly it was that July saw in Charlie, as Will smoothly ducked yet another wildly swinging tent pole. The man was a walking disaster.

As if July could read her mind, she refocused her eyes and looked at Erica with a smile. At that moment Charlie stumbled over his shoelaces. His knees buckled and he pitched forward, all the way to the ground. Without losing a beat, he somersaulted swiftly back up to his feet and continued walking toward the van.

"He's a royal klutz, isn't he?" she asked good-naturedly, and grinned at the flabbergasted Erica. "Oh, it's okay. It's hard to hide that kind of thing from people. But I will say this for the guy—" she giggled and winked at Erica "—he's one excellent lover."

Erica gazed out the window in disbelief at Charlie, who appeared to have caught his belt on the car door. Glancing at July, she took one look at her mischievous expression and burst out laughing. She liked this woman.

"Well, I can imagine that would make up for a lot of broken furniture."

"It does," July agreed.

"Ugh!" Something cold and wet nudged Erica's ankle under the table. As she bent to discover what it could be, she heard July explain.

"Oh, that's just Huck. Short for Huckleberry Hound. Come here, Huck," she called, snapping her fingers.

Huck's tail flopped listlessly across Erica's foot. His plaintive cry told her he wouldn't be coming out anytime soon. He appeared ancient to Erica. He had so much extra skin she couldn't even place his breed. Some kind of big, smelly, watery-eyed...dog. He slobbered affectionately on Erica's foot for a while, before drifting noisily off to sleep. She hadn't known that dogs snored. And so loudly.

"Well, that's okay." July shrugged. "You'll get to meet him soon enough. He's a funny dog, that one. He just loves rocks. Digs 'em up, chews on 'em, chases 'em when you throw them and catches them, no matter how big, in his mouth. Weird. But anyway, that's why he has so many broken teeth—" she was in the process of explaining, when the kids came screaming into the house.

"Mommm! Dad just shut his hand in the garage door! Get the ice!"

July sighed. "Be right there."

Charlie's fingers, although somewhat flatter and darker in color, were unbroken. Under the scrutiny of Will's and July's curious gazes, Erica examined him, and pronounced him fit to drive.

The kids decided to ride with the Martins in their roomy van, and Will and Erica got custody of Huck. Lifting his head, the old hound yawned hugely, blowing a foul wind into the front seat.

"Oh, my word! What is that disgusting smell?" Erica wrinkled her nose and glanced at Will once they were on the road again.

"Don't look at me!" He laughed and rolled down his window.

The dog. It had to be. "Huck?" Erica leaned over the back seat and gazed into his watery eyes. His tail lifted tiredly in greeting, and he whimpered tragically and yawned another jaw-cracking yawn.

"Oh, Huck!" There it was again. She unrolled her window. "Will, do you think he's carsick?"

"I don't know. You're the medic."

Erica looked over her shoulder to see if he was teasing.

Will laughed. "He smells like he's dying."

"I wonder if we should pull over and get him a rock or something. July says he loves rocks."

"Let's wait. If he gets any worse, we'll stop at a store and buy him some mouthwash. I'm willing to try anything to cure that problem."

When the air cleared, they rolled their windows back up and smiled at each other. Will had been delighted when the kids chose to ride with their cousins. Now he had Emily all to himself for the next hour or so.

"Where'd you learn so much about first aid?" Will asked.

"Oh, uh, that," Erica frantically searched for a plausible explanation. "I, uh, watch a lot of 'General Hospital.'"

He lifted an eyebrow in surprise. "That's amazing."

Anxious to change the subject, Erica asked, "Where exactly do we go from here?"

"For now we drive. At least another hour or so. Then, when we get to Ruby River, we unload the vehicles into three rafts that are there waiting for us. We leave the car and the van with the shuttle service. They'll drive them downriver to another lot for us. We'll pick them up in three days."

"Have you done this before?"

"Camping? Yes. I think I'm the only one who's ever been rafting before, though. We used to go camping together all the time, before, well, before June died. This is the first time we've gone since then."

"Oh, Will. I'm so sorry," she murmured, her chin resting on the back of the car seat as she patted old Huck on the head.

"It's okay." He reached over and ran his fingers lightly across her cheek. "I know she would have wanted us to keep going together, for the kids' sakes. They love it. And after we all discussed it, we figured we'd like to try something a little different this year. That's why we decided to go rafting."

"Oh." She smiled at Huck's soulful expression. He loved having his head scratched.

"Don't worry about..." Will shrugged and glanced over at her.

She stopped scratching Huck and turned to look at him. "What?"

"About, you know, taking June's place, or fitting in or anything...."

How did he know? Erica smiled.

"They are all really glad you're coming. I can tell that July and Charlie like you a lot. And of course it goes without saying that our kids think you're great. Theirs will, too. And, well, I think you're pretty great myself...."

"Oh." Erica smiled into his sexy green eyes, and felt a delicious thrill run up her spine. *Our kids.* It had a nice ring. "Oh!" She wrinkled her nose.

Will's heart sank. What had he said? She looked so repelled.

"Oh, Huck!" she cried, and frantically rolled down her window. "Stop yawning! Bad boy!"

Huck whimpered and slowly wagged his tail.

Chapter Six

"What did you say Charlie did for a living?" Erica asked Will as she watched the Martin van overshoot the entrance to the vehicle shuttle-service parking lot. The van lurched into reverse and, tires spinning, catapulted back to the entrance. Once there, it bounced across the lot—narrowly missing Will's car—and finally screeched to a halt.

"He teaches navigation for the air force in Sacramento," Will said calmly, and released the cords that held their camping gear in place.

Erica joined him at the back of the trailer. "That's what I thought you said...." Her face registered mild surprise.

"Can't find his way out of a wet paper bag on the ground." Will grinned. "But they say he's hot stuff in the air."

"Must have something to do with the altitude," Erica mused, as Charlie fell out of the van and stumbled across the pavement to meet them. July slid open the passenger door and the kids tumbled into the lot in an excited bundle of arms and legs.

"Come on, you guys," Will called, rounding up the kids. "The rafts are already tied up at the dock and we need to load them as quickly as possible. If we don't hurry, I'm afraid we may run out of daylight." He glanced at his watch. "We're already running a little late."

Will and Erica climbed into the trailer and began passing out backpacks and sleeping bags to be carried to the dock. From there, some of the supplies would be loaded into the two passenger rafts. A third, smaller, raft would be towed along to carry the dry goods.

Once the supplies had been stowed in the various rafts, Will and Charlie passed out the life preservers. The kids ran around the dock in an ecstatic frenzy, having an impromptu pillow fight with their bright-orange jackets.

"No, no, no," Will murmured, coming up to Erica, oblivious to the chaos behind him. He pulled the belt out of her hands. "Like this." Grinning wolfishly, he reached around her waist and threaded the belt through its loops. When he had finished with all her ties, he chucked her under the chin. "There you go, little girl."

"Thanks, mister," Erica teased, and pinched him playfully on the cheek.

They'd had a wonderful time together in the car, getting to know each other on the way to the river. That is, with the exception of Huck's apparent car-sickness problem. But even that seemed to run its course, leaving them to enjoy each other's company without interruption.

Although at one point Erica had been taken off guard by a curious comment Will made regarding the men in her life. He seemed almost jealous of some mysterious man she might be dating in San Francisco. She did her best to reassure him that there was no one, and that she truly had been with her family the weekend she'd been gone. His obvious relief pleased her, and for the rest of the trip, they'd talked about his orchards, the kids, their tastes in music, favorite movies and dozens of other things they discovered they had in common. Will's belief systems closely mirrored her own, causing her to wonder how he and Emily would ever get along for any length of time. Well, she had enough to worry about without adding that burden to her load.

Will reached out and tweaked the end of her nose. "I wouldn't want anything to happen to my favorite nanny," he said, and straightened her life jacket.

"You only like me because I shave my mustache." She smiled beguilingly up at him.

"You got me," he said with a laugh.

Samantha stood awkwardly off to the side, watching the biplay between the two adults.

"Dad?" she called. "Us girls are gonna ride with Aunt July and Uncle Charlie. The boys want to ride with you, okay?"

"Sure, honey." Will nodded in agreement.

Sam stared at them for a moment longer, before moving off to join her cousins.

"Is everyone wearing a life jacket? Yes? Good. Let's go!" Will commanded, and began assisting the various parties to their rafts. "Okay, everybody. Time to shove off." Will's voice was filled with boyish enthusiasm.

Erica cocked her head in the direction of the parking lot. "Will? What's that sound?"

A pitiful howl echoed from the vicinity of their car.

"We forgot Huck!" she cried, making a grab for the dock.

"I'll get him." Will sighed and climbed out of the raft.

Moments later Huck came bounding down the hill, toward the river, just ahead of Will. Joyfully barking at his strange orange family, he plunged off the edge of the dock and paddled around in the water, yowling with delight.

"Come on, Huck. Here boy!" the kids yelled, beckoning the old hound into a raft. Huck swam to the shore and dug up a large rock and carried it in his mouth, careering down the dock. With a flying leap—admirable for a dog half his age—he landed with a thud in Erica and Will's raft.

He dropped his rock and shook his coat, first cranking up his head and then letting the momentum carry throughout his body, ending with his flailing tail. Smelly drops of river water, tainted by Huck's particular aroma, flew in all directions, soaking everyone.

"Oh, Huck," Erica moaned. Taking her words as high praise, Huck passionately slobbered on Erica's cheek, turned around half a dozen times and settled comfortably on her feet.

"Okay, *now* we're ready to go," Will shouted, and shoving away from the dock, they moved out into the river.

"Wa, wa, wa, whoooaaaa!" Charlie yelled, his raft spinning in slow circles about thirty yards behind Will's raft.

From where Erica sat, reclining comfortably against the wall of her raft, she could hear July and the girls laughing and squealing as Charlie tried to maneuver their raft out of a whirlpool near the shore.

"Will?" she asked sleepily, lifting her straw hat off her face.

"Hmm?" Will opened one eye and smiled at her from where he lay, sprawled out next to her.

"Maybe we should go give them a hand," she mumbled.

"Nah," he said, sitting up to check on Charlie and the girls. "He's got it under control."

"Whatever you say," she returned agreeably. "Pass me some sunscreen will you?"

"Just a sec," he said, rummaging through her backpack. The boys and Huck lay in a lazy lump, arms and legs dangling in the water, and munched on junk food while they laughed at the girls.

Muscle-melting heat beat down from the cloudless blue sky, putting them all in a lethargic, happy-go-lucky mood. Sun-dappled leaves swayed and danced in the light summer

breeze, casting spotty patterns on the river's clear water.
Erica felt marvelous. She couldn't remember feeling this
alive, this completely relaxed and happy.

As unobtrusively as possible, she peeked under the brim
of her floppy hat and watched Will search for her suntan
lotion. Yep, she thought, enjoying the view. He looked great
in a pair of bathing trunks. Unlike poor Charlie there, who
had to wear a T-shirt and baseball hat for fear of burning to
a crisp.

"Here we go." Will held out the sunscreen and then,
changing his mind, poured some into the palm of his hand.
"Allow me," he whispered. Scooting over to where she lay,
he smoothed the lotion on her back and shoulders, cover-
ing every inch that was not protected by her brightly flowered bikini.

Erica stretched languidly, enjoying the feel of his hands
as he massaged the lotion into her skin. "Where'd you learn
to do this? You're very good," she purred and turned over
to allow him access to the front.

"Ah. Well, I majored in suntans at Cal State," he said
modestly, and squeezed a dollop onto her stomach. "Many
people don't know that there is an art to achieving the perfect tan."

"Oh?"

"Yeah, it's called skipping horticulture." Smoothing the
lotion across her flat tummy, over her hip and down her
thigh, he let his hands linger where they had normally had
no business lingering. So what? he thought, throwing himself into the moment. So it was just an excuse to grope her
fabulous body. What she didn't know wouldn't hurt her....
No—he swallowed a groan—it would probably just kill him.
Will felt like a kid in a candy store as he slathered her from
top to delectable bottom. He knew that even the most de-
termined UV ray couldn't penetrate *this* coat of sunscreen.
With a Herculean effort at nonchalance, he finished with a
pat on her hip and snapped the cap back onto the bottle.

"Here, let me do you." Erica sat up and took the bottle from his hand. "I'll show you how it's done at, ah, um, UCLA." Her hands trembled violently and her heart thudded against her flowered bikini top. She'd almost said her alma mater, Stanford. Will knew Emily was studying for her doctorate in sociology at UCLA. He just didn't know that she was...doing it at the moment. She took a deep, calming breath.

Shaking her head over her near miss, she squeezed a line of lotion across Will's broad shoulders and began to rub it in. Her hands flowed easily over his strong back and down the contours of his work-hardened arms. She loved the sensation of his heated flesh, like satin beneath her fingertips. Erica massaged his smooth, hard muscles for as long as she dared, and with great reluctance, declared herself finished.

"Good technique," Will murmured. "You've studied hard."

"Yeah, well, I missed a spot," she teased, rubbing some lotion into the stubbled spot she'd shaved bald at the back of his head.

"Hey, now!" Will grabbed her wrist and pulled her across his knees. Squealing with laughter, she struggled to sit up. Huck started barking, and before she knew it she was fending off giggling boys and a slobbering tongue. She only hoped the latter belonged to Huck. Just as she was beginning to fear that they would capsize, Charlie and the girls pulled up alongside their raft.

"Ahoy, there!" he yodeled, as he steered his raft into theirs. Poor Charlie was already neon pink from the elbows and knees down. The back of his neck looked as though it were on fire, as did his ears and nose.

"Hey, Charlie," Will yelled, and tossed the sunscreen into his lap. "Put this on, will you? Before you spontaneously combust."

"Thanks, buddy." He fumbled with the lotion until July took it from his hands and opened it for him. "Some

weather we're having, huh?'' he commented as his wife
covered his ears and nose with sunscreen.

"Yeah. I just hope it lasts."

"Oh, it should. Hey, Will. According to my map, we're
almost at the first campsite." Charlie dug a large, unwieldy
map out of his back pocket and spread it out on the rounded
edge of the raft. "My guess is we'll get there in about fif-
teen or twenty minutes."

"Good." Will looked at his watch. "That will give us
plenty of time to pitch the tents."

They finally arrived, after several misguided directions
from Charlie, at the first campsite. Soaked, but happy after a vigorous water fight, they floated into the eddy where
they would lash the rafts for the night. The water was far too
fast at the campsite side, but as luck would have it, there was
a giant old fir tree lying on its side that would serve perfectly as a bridge across the swirling water.

One by one, Will carried the kids across the river, releas-
ing them joyfully into the woods. July and Erica carted
boxes of food and cookware across once the kids were out
of the way, and Will helped Charlie with some of the larger
items—cook stove, the kids' tent and other sundry items.
Soon all that was left were their personal belongings.

It was such a beautiful day, the magnificence of the
wooded campsite was profound. Erica pulled in a lungful of
fresh, pure, pine-scented air and was nearly overcome by the
splendor of it all. She stood watching the children cavort,
taking pleasure in their silly games, knowing how it felt to
be giddy with excitement.

"Having fun?" Will stood behind her and gently
squeezed her arms. Looking up over her shoulder, she
smiled up at him and had to fight the urge to kiss his soft,
sensuous lips.

"Um-hmm." She nodded, and could tell by the expression in his eyes that his thoughts mirrored her own.

He let his hands slide down her arm, and he twined his fingers with hers. "Come on." He tugged her along with him. "Let's go get our tents and sleeping bags."

Erica followed Will slowly back across the giant fir tree and tried not to glance down at the rushing water below. Arriving at the supply raft, she donned her backpack, picked up the tent that Will pointed out and headed up to the tree bridge. Charlie trundled along behind her, carrying only his pack. As they approached the middle of the tree, Erica felt a pole begin to slip, and stopped to adjust her load.

"Here, Emily, let me give you a hand there." Ever the gentleman, Charlie offered his assistance. Reaching awkwardly around Erica, he attempted to relieve her of her burden.

Having seen him in action, and having no wish to be knocked off the old tree into the rapidly moving water, Erica politely declined his offer of help. "Oh, no, thanks, Charlie. I have it now."

In the spirit of chivalry, Charlie felt duty-bound to insist. "Really, I don't mind. Allow me." He grabbed the ends of her tent poles.

Still dubious, Erica had to decline. "No, no, that's okay. Really, I have it," she said, and tried to slip the tent poles out of Charlie's well-meaning grasp.

"I got it," he grunted, listing dangerously backward.

"No, I've got it," Erica gasped, feeling herself leaning precariously with him.

"Oh, come on now," he cajoled, not realizing how far over he was leaning. "I don't mind—" Charlie stepped back and for some reason, peculiar only to him, lost his balance. Lunging at Erica's tent poles for support, he snatched them out of her hands and, spinning wildly, launched her tent and its poles into the rapidly flowing river.

"Oh, my!" Erica breathed, as she watched her tent swim out to sea, where it would eventually spawn with all the other tents Charlie had no doubt set free.

Unable to resist an opportunity to chase a large, tent-shaped rock, Huck ran to the middle of the old fir tree and, much to everyone's horror, jumped in to retrieve Erica's AWOL shelter.

Paddling as fast as his ancient arthritic legs would allow, Huck valiantly swam after the tent, amid the screams and pandemonium that ensued on the shore. But alas, the tent was younger and faster, and Huck, much to his sorrow, lost the battle. Paddling to the shore, Huck shook his coat and howled.

"Uh-oh" was all Charlie could manage, his face seven shades of crimson.

"No biggie, Charlie," Erica said sympathetically. "Those things happen."

"Yeah, but why always to me?" Charlie hung his head, embarrassed."

"Oh, come on now, Chuckie, old boy." Will strolled across the tree to join them above the water. "It's not the end of the world. Emily can sleep in my tent." He wiggled his eyebrows suggestively at her. "In fact, you may have done me a big favor," he said, and hooted with glee.

Erica elbowed Will in the ribs. "I most certainly cannot sleep with you in your tent," she hissed.

"Well, you don't have to get huffy about it." He grinned. "Okay, okay. You can sleep in my tent and I'll sleep by the fire. That way I can keep an eye out for bears."

"Bears?" Erica asked, her eyes wide with fear.

"Big." Will nodded solemnly.

"Sounds like a plan." She smiled brightly at Charlie. "I'll take the tent, and Will can watch for...bears." She shivered.

"Well, if you're sure..." Charlie perked up slightly.

"We're sure," Erica assured him with a pat on his back.

"Okay." Will clapped his hands once and rubbed them together. "Now that that's settled, let's make camp."

"Is he going to be okay?" Will looked up as Erica came through the flap of her tent.

She crawled over and sat down next to Will as he pumped up her air mattress with a hand pump. "Oh, yeah, just another small bump on his head. Now he has a matched set." She rolled her eyes expressively.

"What happened?" he asked, gripping the mattress and testing it for firmness.

"July says he was walking along the path, berating himself for losing my tent, and walked smack-dab into a tree. I wrapped his head and he's resting comfortably with an ice pack."

"Boy, that 'General Hospital' must be some show," he commented dryly. Deciding the mattress was perfect, Will capped it off and spread Erica's sleeping bag out on top.

"Um-hmm." Erica was noncommittal. "Will...are there really bears out there?"

Will sported the same crooked grin Danny wore when he was torturing his sister. "Nah, I was just kidding. I wanted to make sure you took my tent."

The light was beginning to fade, back under the trees where they had chosen to set up camp. Erica's luminous eyes fairly glowed in the early twilight. Her incredibly silky, straight brown hair was pulled back in a loose ponytail. And sitting there in an old sweatshirt and torn-up jeans, she looked almost as young as Sam. But there was nothing fatherly in the thoughts that coursed through Will's mind as his eyes caressed her smooth, clear complexion and lingered momentarily on the lip she was so thoughtfully chewing.

"If that's true, then I don't mind sleeping outside. Really. I feel terrible about taking your tent. This is your trip. You should be comfortable."

"Hey." Will looked wounded. "This is your trip, too. And furthermore, I won't hear another word about you sleeping outside. You're in here and that's final."

Secretly relieved, she nodded in compliance. "Will?"

"Hmm?"

"Why did Charlie set up all the tents so far apart?"

Will chuckled. "Oh, I suppose for several reasons. One being, a tent filled to bursting with six excited kids is a noisy tent. And two... Well, let's just say Charlie and July like their privacy, which—" his lips curled mischievously "—can also mean a... noisy tent."

"Oh. Then it's true," Erica murmured, thinking back on her conversation with July earlier that day. She made the mistake of glancing up and catching Will's eye. The little tent seemed suddenly smaller and she looked away, embarrassed.

"What's true?"

"Oh, nothing," she hedged. She couldn't bring herself to tell Will that July's klutzy husband was reported to be a veritable Baryshnikov between the sheets. At least that explained the huge, triangular campsite. She hadn't liked being so far away from the others, but if what Will said was true, then she would relish her solitude.

Will had finished his tasks, and knew that he should be leaving, but as always, something about the appealing way she twisted her hair around her finger, the gentle curve of her smile, the slender dip at her waist, held him captive. He chattered on, searching for an excuse—any excuse—to stay. The rest of the world seemed to fall away, leaving the two of them completely alone in the intimate confines of the tiny tent.

"You should be comfortable on this," he said, thumping the mattress with his fist. She nodded slowly and his heart picked up speed. "I... ah, have one just like it, you know, out there."

"Will you be warm enough?"

The concern in her voice thrilled him and he felt his ears turn red with pleasure. "Oh, sure," he asserted manfully. "These old goose-down bags are the best. Used to take 'em up north, into the mountains to hunt in the fall. Even on the days it froze, I'd stay nice and warm." He stretched his arms casually above his head.

His artless ramblings brought a smile to her lips. He was trying to impress her. And it was working.

"Oh, Daddy!"

Sam's call interrupted their quiet moment.

"In here," Will yelled. To Erica he said, "Now, don't waste another minute feeling bad about staying in here. First of all, it wasn't your fault that your tent escaped." He laughed. "And second, I'll be fine out there. Just fine."

"What are you guys doing in here?" Sam asked, poking her head through the flap. She glanced over at Erica, her pretty face marred by a vulnerable frown.

"Just helping Emily get settled."

"Oh." She crawled inside and squeezed between the two adults. Looking up at her dad, she said, "Aunt July wants you to make a fire so she can start dinner. And—" she swung her gaze over to Erica "—Danny won't leave us alone." Her lower lip protruded petulantly.

"Are you and Rachel excluding him?"

"Why does he always have to hang around us?"

"Probably because Rachel is his cousin too, and he likes being around you guys. Give him a break, Sam." Erica ruffled the young girl's curly mop. "He just wants to be with you. Sometimes it seems like the big kids are having all the fun."

Will's heart swelled as he saw the ease with which Emily handled Sam's complaints. In no time she had Sam giggling and comfortable again. Will knew that his relationship with Emily worried Sam, and he couldn't blame her. It worried him somewhat, too. In the two years that June had been gone, he hadn't given much thought to bringing another woman into their lives. But watching the two of them together, he began to wonder if maybe it wasn't time.

Bustling busily at the camp stove, July had the evening meal of hot dogs and potato salad under control. The kids were playing cards by the fire and the men were sitting on a couple of camp stools, talking about the orchard business. After several cups of July's camp coffee, Erica was beginning to wonder where the ladies' room might be located. Not in any huge hurry, she decided to wait for a break in the men's conversation and ask Will privately where she could find the rest room.

"How are the nuts this year, Will?" Charlie had taken off his hat and shirt and was rubbing some salve onto his neon farmer's tan. His lily-white torso and forehead were stylishly complemented by his crimson red face, neck, forearms and calves. It was painful just to look at him.

Will poked at the fire with a stick. "Can't complain."

"Thinking about cleaning and drying your own someday?"

"Maybe. I know several people who do. It's a big decision." Stretching his legs, Will propped his feet up on a rock.

"That reminds me. July wanted me to get some nuts this year. Says she can use them at Christmastime."

"No problem."

Erica did her best to swallow her mirth. Their conversation tickled her funny bone. To anyone who didn't know Will grew hazelnuts, the topic would have seemed bizarre. An errant giggle erupted past her pursed lips, and she looked up and caught the amusement in Will's eyes. His lazy wink told her he knew what she'd been thinking. She grinned. They were getting to know each other pretty well, she thought contentedly. She motioned to him with her head to join her. Standing and stretching, Will excused himself from Charlie and ambled over to where she stood.

"I was just wondering where the ladies' room might be."
She glanced uncertainly around the campsite. "Did we bring
one with us?"

Will regarded her large, curious eyes with humor. "Yep.
We brought something." His lips twitched mischievously.

He was up to something. She could tell by the way he was
trying not to laugh. Leading her over to a box of supplies
that was covered by a large tarp, he rummaged around inside and finally came up with a roll of toilet paper and
pointed to the woods.

"Do you mean to tell me that *that* is the bathroom?" She
looked, eyes round, at the shadowy forest with obvious dis-
taste.

"Yep."

"Charming," she muttered, and frowned at Will for a
moment, trying to decide if he was joking. He wasn't.

"You want me to go with you?"

The thought was much more horrifying than going alone.
"Uh, no, thank you. I'll manage," she said brightly, and
went off in search of Huck. At least he might be some protection from things that went bump in the woods. Although Will had assured her several times that there were no
animals more dangerous than Bambi out there, she wasn't
wild about going completely alone.

"Here, boy! Come on, Huck!" she called to the wrinkled pile of skin and bones. Grunting, Huck lifted his tail
once and let it fall lifelessly to the ground. Clearly he was
down for the count. Oh, well, she would just have to go it
alone.

Having no desire to expose her derriere to a bunch of
giggling kids, she decided to hike up the hill, behind their
campsite, in search of the perfect, secluded but safe, spot to
accomplish her business. Gingerly she picked her way over
fallen logs and assorted bushes, using low branches to help
pull herself up the hill. She wasn't in the stellar cardio con-
dition that she'd always thought. Breathless, she tore off a

length of toilet paper from the roll and mopped her brow.
It was eerie out there by herself. She almost wished she'd
taken Will up on his offer to come with her.

That's strange, she thought, trudging farther up the hill
and squinting into the darkening sky. That big brown lump
about fifty feet away seemed to have moved just now. She
stopped moving and watched for a while. Nah, must just be
her overactive imagination.

There it was again! This time she wasn't so sure she'd
imagined it. Slowly she approached the mystery rock, hoping against hope it wasn't Gentle Ben—or worse yet, not so
Gentle Ben.

She moved. The rock moved. She stopped. The rock
stopped. *This was no rock. No way was this a rock.* No, she
thought, her eyes glazing over with terror, unless rocks stood
up on their hind legs and sniffed the wind.

Adrenaline flowed through her body. Her heart thundered in her ears and she forgot to breathe. Sweating, shivering, shaking, she wondered frantically what to do next.

Should she climb a tree? Play dead? Run for her life?
Without realizing it, her legs took over and were suddenly
pumping her down the hill faster than she'd ever traveled
before. She hurtled over berry vines, dodged trees, flew over
stumps, her legs two pistons firing her back to camp.

"Will!" she shrieked, eyes wild, hair flying.

Everyone ran to see the screaming banshee come tearing
into camp. Erica's legs didn't stop moving until she landed
in Will's strong arms.

"What the hell happened?" he asked, his heart pounding nearly as hard as hers. He pulled her tightly to his chest
and held her close. Rocking her back and forth, he stroked
her hair and rubbed her back.

"I think...huh...huh—" she puffed "—I saw...
huh...huh—" she huffed "—a b-b-*bear!*"

The kids all screamed at the top of their lungs and ran
around in frightened circles.

"Kids!" he bellowed, and the screaming abruptly stopped. Not wanting to alarm the happy campers any more than necessary, he said, "Oh, honey, I don't think you saw a bear. A deer, maybe, but not a bear."

"Will! I know what I saw and this was no Smoky the Deer!" she shouted up at him, her nose bumping into his.

More screaming and circles came from the kids.

"Quiet!" he thundered, and the screaming stopped again. "You kids all go wash up for dinner. Now!" he ordered when they just stood there staring, agog with the delicious terror of it all. Moaning and groaning, they shuffled off to do as they were told.

"Oh, Will," she breathed, and attempted to pick the brambles out of her hair. "There is no way that I'm going back out there by myself."

Still crushing her in his arms, he kissed her lightly on the forehead. "You don't have to, sweetheart. Hang on just a sec, and I'll go with you.".

Will led her over to the fire and then went to where they'd stacked the supplies. He rummaged through his pack, and came up with a box of bullets and a deadly looking rifle. Quickly loading the gun, he tucked it under his arm and went over to where she still stood, quaking in her sandals.

"Ready?"

"No?"

"Sweetheart," Will said gently, "don't worry. Whatever it was is probably long gone by now. Besides . . . I won't let anything happen to you."

Looking up into his rugged face, now etched with concern, she believed him. She wasn't afraid of much of anything, as long as Will was there, she was amazed to discover. How was it that by the sheer power of his self-confidence, she felt able to go back out there and face a bear? Somehow, in her mind Will was bigger and stronger than that bear.

Unconsciously she tucked her hand into the crook of
Will's steely arm. He tightened his bicep to squeeze her hand
and reassure her that she had nothing to fear.

"Do you still have the toilet paper?" he whispered down
at her.

Mutely she held up the mangled roll for his inspection.

He nodded and steered her to the edge of the woods.

"Will?"

"Hmm?"

"Uh, don't stand too close now," she instructed him
shyly.

"I won't."

"But, um, don't stand too far away, either...."

"I won't."

"And, Will?" she giggled. "The bear is brown. I'll be the
pink one, so be careful."

Will laughed.

Chapter Seven

The sun had set and the campfire crackled and popped merrily in the dark. Excited by the long, flickering shadows, the kids chased one another, taking turns being Erica's bear, and scaring themselves silly.

Appetites ravenous, everyone had gustily consumed mass quantities of potato salad, chips, hot dogs and soda pop. Everyone, that is, with the exception of Charlie, who was still artfully preparing his hot-dog bun.

"There's a science to this," he said defensively, self-conscious at the attention he was getting from the three adults, who sat watching his meticulous ministrations.

Perfectly placed pickles, the strategic arrangement of onions, mustard that zigged, catsup that zagged—it was truly a sight to behold.

"Good buns are definitely important," he explained, "but the real key to success is starting with the perfect hot dog."

Will lifted a smart-aleck eyebrow at Erica and tried to hold back a laugh.

Ignoring him, Charlie pulled his roasting stick from the fire and held it triumphantly in the air. "I ask you, is this a perfect hot dog or what?"

"Bravo!" Will and the ladies saluted him with their soda cans.

"And now..." Charlie said, slipping the tube steak off his stick and onto his bun, "I shall demonstrate how to eat a masterpiece." He smiled modestly at his audience.

"Drumroll, please." Will grabbed a plastic knife and fork and beat on the bottom of a metal pail.

"It's all in the wrist." Picking up the large, slippery sandwich, Charlie opened his mouth to sample his culinary expertise. Unfortunately his grip was a little too firm, and his perfect hot dog chose that precise moment to shoot out the back end of the bun and land in Huck's open mouth.

"Quite the technique you have there," Will noted dryly as Huck trotted away, the hot dog in question bobbing out the corners of his satisfied grin.

Soda sprayed out of Erica's mouth as the humor of the situation caught her unawares. She mopped at her shirt with a paper napkin and tried to stop laughing. But the flabbergasted expression on poor Charlie's face was just too much.

"That was the last one, too," he muttered, and tossed his bun on the fire.

"It's okay, honey. I'll make you a tuna sandwich." July patted her husband on his knee.

"I don't want a tuna sandwich!" he complained, as petulant as one of the kids.

Biting the inside of her cheek so hard she feared it would bleed, Erica stood and excused herself. "I...uh...am going to run to the river now. For some dishwater," she spluttered, and grabbing the empty pail, sprinted down the long path to the river. She was laughing so hard that she didn't hear Will come up behind her.

"Hey!" he said gruffly, and grabbed her by the arm, spinning her around to face him. "Show some respect! The man just lost his hot dog." Will could keep a straight face no longer.

They fell into each other's arms and howled.

"Poor Charlie," she gasped. "As if he doesn't have enough problems with those two attractive bumps on his head."

"Oh, and let's not forget that fabulous suntan he picked up today."

"Ooo, stop!" Erica panted, and gripped the front of his shirt. "You're killing me! Besides, this isn't very nice." She fell against him in another fit of laughter.

"Okay, no more jokes," he agreed, still laughing as hard as she was.

Erica wiped her eyes and nose on his shirt.

"Hey," he complained, looking down at his soggy shirt.

"Sorry," she giggled. "Here." Pulling her shirttail out of her shorts, she offered it up to him. "Just don't blow."

"Come on." He took the pail from her and started down the path. "Let's go get some water before they start wondering what happened to us." Taking her hand in his, he quickly led her, stumbling behind him, over the smooth river stones and down to the beach. She felt as giddy as one of the kids. Must be all the sugary soda pop. Couldn't be the man. The man whose large, strong, sexy hands pulled her farther and farther from the safety of camp. "Uh, Will?" Giggling, she tripped over a large wobbly stone and lunged at him for support.

"What?" he asked, catching her and righting her at his side.

"Uh—" She was breathless. "Uh, could we slow down? These aren't my hiking sandals." She held her foot up.

"Oh, sorry." He bent down and angled his broad shoulder into her abdomen. Before she knew what was happening, Will had thrown her over his shoulder and was striding rapidly down to the river.

Too stunned to protest, Erica could do nothing but laugh as she watched the world go by upside down. Slipping her hands in his back pockets for support, she kicked her legs happily in the air and battled a bad case of the hiccups.

Will stopped walking and looked under his arm at her face, her hair was draped like a silk scarf on the ground. "I know a surefire cure for the hiccups."

"I just, *hic,* bet you do." Gripping his arm, she pulled her face up to his. "What is it? Scaring the, *hic,* heck out of me? Forget it."

"Okay... You're the one who's suffering. Not me." He swatted her playfully on the bottom.

"*Hic*— Ha! They'll go away as soon as you put me down." she gasped and pounded on his derriere in return. And what a nice, firm little tush it was, too, she mused. Even if it was, *hic,* upside down.

"Upsy-daisy," he grunted, and set her on the ground next to a huge weeping willow whose long branches danced and bobbed in the rippling river.

Hiccupping noisily, Erica stood under the leafy cathedral with Will's arm around her shoulders and looked up through the branches into the sky. Large, puffy white clouds floated lazily past the moon and frogs croaked melodically. The evening breeze—mercifully cooler now—caused the treetops to sway, and the river's gentle roar lulled her into a peculiar intimacy with Will. Glancing up at him, she found him studying her, an enigmatic expression across his handsome face.

He shook his head and grinned, and Erica wondered what he'd been thinking. Were his thoughts similar to her own? If so, they were in trouble.

Will set to work filling the pail with water. "You know," he said, waxing nostalgic, "this brings back so many memories."

"I'm sure, *hic,* it must." It was strange to realize that the last time he'd done this, it had been June standing at his side. The thought made her feel sorry for him. And for June. And, oddly enough, for herself, and the years that they had all lost with each other.

"The kids sure seem to be having a great time." He smiled at the carefree hollering that echoed through the woods, as he dipped the pail into the rapidly flowing river.

Erica nodded. "Even *Hic* . . . er, Huck seems to be enjoying himself." She helped him lift the pail out of the water and swing it up onto the beach. "I think."

Will smiled and looked over at her. "You ever think about having kids?"

Though she was still hiccupping loudly, her eyes darted up to his. *I already have two,* she wanted to say, but realizing that was absurd replied, "Um-hmm. I think about it." And to her complete and utter amazement, she found that she was telling the truth. Until this summer, she hadn't thought she even liked kids, and now here she was, loving his.

"I wanted several more. So did June," Will confessed. He picked up the heavy pail and his eyes pulled hers toward him.

"I know," she said sympathetically. For a moment, the barrier was down and Erica could see the raw grief and self-blame Will carried for a situation that was beyond his control. Desperately she wished that there were something she could do to ease his burden, to soothe his pain. But she knew that only time would heal Will. Just as quickly as she'd glimpsed his torment, it was gone.

The roar of the river seemed to grow louder, and neither Will nor Erica could summon the wherewithal to tear their eyes away from each other. The explosive chemistry that only the two of them were able to generate together was back, stronger than ever. They stared at each other in confusion, each knowing that they were courting disaster—she because of Emily, and he because it was still too soon for Sam.

"We should probably, *hic*—"

Water sloshed out of the pail as Will unceremoniously dropped it on the beach and pulled her into his arms. Before she knew what had hit her, he was kissing the breath right out of her. Stunned, she simply stood, limp as a rag doll, arms dangling at her sides, and let him work his magic on her mouth.

"Well?"

He moved away from her lips and sought her throat with his mouth, sending high volts of sensation clear to her toes. Tangling his hands in her hair, he pulled her head to the side and nibbled his way up her neck to her ear.

"Well?" he repeated.

"Well, well, well..." she breathed blankly, angling her head to give him better access to the place where her shoulder met her neck. "Well, what?"

"Did it work?"

"Did what work?"

"Do you still have the hiccups?"

She stopped and thought for a moment. "Uh, no. How about that."

"I told you I have a surefire cure for the hiccups."

"Wow. That's great. I'd love to see how you cure the flu."

"Ah, well now." He ruffled her hair good-naturedly. "We'd have to be married for me to show you that."

"Oh." His words brought a myriad of emotions to the surface. Emotions she didn't want to deal with here...now. She shivered.

"Hey. You're getting cold." He bent to pick up the pail of water. "Let's get you back to the campfire."

Will was right. It was getting chilly, but that's not why she was shivering. He moved back onto the shadowy path before her and headed toward camp.

Erica watched him walk away—this man she wanted so badly and could never have—and appreciated the fluid masculinity of his stride, the breadth of his strong shoulders, his easy air of confidence.

With a bittersweet ache in her heart, she realized that unfortunately for her, Will Spencer always had and always would belong to someone else.

They'd been telling stories around the campfire, and it was Will's turn. The kids sat with rapt attention as he spun his tale of old-fashioned, skin-crawling, ghost-haunting, bear-eating campfire horror. And always, just before the story got too spooky, Will would say or do something that would have them all screaming with laughter.

Every so often, as she sat across the fire from him with little Noah in her lap, Will would catch her eye, and her heart would leap at his sexy wink. The sparks were flying, and not just from the campfire. She loved the way he interacted with the kids, teasing them, teaching them. A hollow sense of longing filled Erica as she watched him, a longing that had become a growing void in her heart since the day she first laid eyes on Will.

Before that moment, she'd never known what she was missing by putting her career first. She thought she'd loved jet-setting around with her elderly patient. But no lunch on the Riviera with Mr. Clemmins could compare with hot dogs on the river with Will.

A dull clap of thunder rumbled across the humid summer sky, and all the kids screamed, convinced it was the big bear in Will's story coming to get them. It was growing very late, and as the story ended, the widemouthed yawns were contagious.

After a boisterous round of pit stops at the edge of the woods—complete with much nervous speculation about bottom-biting bears—and a quick scrubbing of teeth over a cold pail of water, the kids were ready for bed. They kissed everyone good-night, then scrambled into their tent, where they lay giggling and whispering in the dark.

Several threats of bodily harm from July finally got the kids settled down, leaving the four adults standing around the campfire.

"Well." Charlie stretched broadly and peered through his broken glasses at July. "I'd say it's about that time, wouldn't you, honey?"

July glanced at her watch. "Goodness." She stared wide-eyed at her wrist. "It's nearly midnight."

"And we have a big day ahead of us tomorrow." He sniffed loudly and pulled his pants up farther under his arms. "Good night all." Charlie saluted jauntily, and turning, promptly stepped into an empty pail on his way to their tent. He clattered and crashed around for a moment as he attempted to free his foot and remain standing at the same time. Finally, with a loud clang, the pail sprang free and Charlie fell through the tent flap and disappeared for the night.

July blew a resigned sigh up at the cloudy sky. "See you in the morning," she whispered, and kissed both Will and Erica on the cheek, before skipping off to join Charlie. "'Night," she called before ducking through the flap.

"'Night," they answered in unison.

"I guess it's about that time for me, too." Erica suddenly felt bashful at being left alone with Will.

"It *is?*" Will joshed and raised his eyebrows in mock surprise.

"Not *that* time." She felt her face grow warm. "You know what I mean."

"I know what he means." Will rolled his eyes at the silly laughter that emanated from the couple's tent. "And if that's what you mean, well, okay, if you insist. Let's go get this over with." He pulled playfully on her arm.

"Will!" What was it about this man that had the laughter bubbling up into her throat every time she turned around? "Knock it off. I have a better idea."

"What could be better than that?"

"Straightening this place up." She knew she was looking for reasons to stay up. She wasn't ready to relinquish his company just yet.

"Oh, I know you don't mean that. Come on, wouldn't you rather go make beautiful music together?"

Several particularly lusty growls came from the direction of the Martin tent.

"Like that?"

"Not exactly." He smiled crookedly at her. "We'd make up our own tune," he said, and drew her to a log over by the fire, where they sat, side by side.

Even though she knew he was teasing her, her heart pounded at the thoughts his words brought to life. She gazed into the green moonlight reflected in his eyes. "You're sure you'll be warm enough?" she asked breathily. The wind had a definite chill and thunder had rumbled more than once since Will had told his story to the children.

"Yeah." His upper lip curled charmingly. "I'll be fine. The fire should keep me from freezing completely to death."

Tossing her hair over her shoulders, she smiled cheekily at him. "You'll just freeze partially to death."

"Um-hmm." He nodded sadly and dropped his forehead against hers. "Unless, of course, you'd like to join me out here and help keep me alive...."

"You're impossible," she giggled, and pushed him away. "Okay, then, if you don't want my help cleaning up, I'm going to turn in. Can I get you anything before I go? I mean, I feel so guilty about taking your tent and everything."

Will pretended to think. "There is one thing..."

"What?"

"A little kiss would probably ease some of that terrible guilt you should be feeling." His smile was fetching.

She hooted. "Will, my hiccups are gone."

"Aw, come on now." He pointed at his cheek. "Right here."

His silly, teasing expression made her laugh. It also made her tingle. All over.

"You don't have the hiccups, either." She knew she should retreat while she still had the strength. "'Night," she sang, and skipped across the campground to her lonely tent.

True, Will thought as he watched her gracefully duck into the tent, he didn't have the hiccups. But he did have one or two other problems, which only she could cure.

Will burned the last of the trash and put away the games and toys left behind by the kids. Lifting the flap to their tent, he was pleased to note that all six were sound asleep, packed in like little sardines.

He pumped up his air mattress, unfolded his sleeping bag, put a clean case on his pillow and finally settled into his bed by the fire, all the while thinking about Emily. And how much he wanted her.

Reaching over, he picked up a roasting stick and poked at the flames with it. Sparks shot up into the air and danced on the stiffening breezes until they disappeared, reminding him again how fleeting life was. June had taught him that. And now, with his daughter growing up so quickly, he began to feel his own mortality.

He flopped back down on his mattress and sighed. Was this how it was always going to be for him? Saying goodbye to the ones he loved? First, sweet June, with her ebony hair and laughing eyes . . . and then Samantha . . . and eventually Danny.

And—his heart twisted painfully at the thought—Emily would be leaving in a few months to go back to school. The first day in two lousy years that he'd even been able to smile was the day that Emily had returned from her weekend in San Francisco. And when she left in the fall, he'd be a wreck all over again. How had he let this happen?

Something raw and powerful had come alive in his gut the moment he'd laid eyes on her, standing all hot and bothered in that gauzy yellow dress. If she'd had any idea how much he wanted to grab her and kiss the daylights out of her at that moment, she'd have run back to Harvest Valley and caught the first bus home. Will groaned miserably and rolled onto his side to face the fire.

The lewd and lascivious sounds of some strange foreplay ritual reached him from the vicinity of the Martins' tent, and Will beat his pillow in frustration.

It wasn't fair, he thought, training a miserable eye on Emily's tent. He wondered what she was doing in there. Probably already in dreamland, just like the kids.

Erica bolted upright on her mattress. What on earth was that? An eerie moan came from somewhere beyond her tent, followed by what sounded like an obscene phone call. A dull clap of thunder off somewhere in the distance underscored the music of the Martins.

Snuggling back down into her sleeping bag, Erica rubbed her icy feet rapidly on the mattress in an effort to warm them up and wondered how Will was doing.

The air had a definite chill, and she could hear the wind rustling through the trees. Will was probably warmer out there by the fire than she was in this poor excuse for a shelter, she thought grumpily.

Huffing indignantly, she turned over on her side and rubbed her hands briskly together between her knees. She'd like to put her hands and feet on Will and show him just how cold it was in his flimsy little tent. Grinning up at the ceiling poles in the dark, she knew that what she really wanted was to simply put her hands and feet on Will.

An unusually strong gust of wind rattled the little tent, and shivering, she zipped her bag up under her throat and hoped she wouldn't blow away like the nannies in *Mary Poppins.*

* * *

Pulling his pillow over his ears, Will attempted to mute out his randy in-laws. It only made his craving for Emily that much more unbearable.

She probably wasn't wasting any time thinking about him, he decided, wondering how she'd liked his cure for the hiccups. Maybe, if he was lucky, they'd come back and she'd ask him to cure her again before the night was over.

He groaned. He had to stop thinking about her. It was driving him out of his cotton-picking mind. He tried counting sheep. Didn't work. A flash of lightning lit the sky and Will counted the seconds till the first clap of thunder. It was still a ways off. Hopefully it would stay there.

His thoughts drifted back to Charlie and July. As happy as he was that they were still crazy for each other after all these years, Will couldn't help but feel lonelier than ever. June had been gone now for over two years, and he'd said his goodbyes and dealt with the pain of that loss. But having Emily less than twenty yards away and not being able to touch her—now *that* was torture. Peeking out from his bag, he could see big, dark, rather ominous clouds rolling across the sky.

Great. Just what he needed. Nature's cold shower. It was then that he felt it. One giant drop of rain hit him smack-dab in the middle of his face. Not wanting to believe that this could be happening, Will looked over at Huck, who was biting the air and rapidly licking his nose. *Damn*. It was raining.

"Uh-oh," he groaned as another huge drop landed on his face and threatened to drown him. Then another...and another...and another...faster and faster, until there were too many to count, pelting him like so many knives and forks from the sky.

It was a cruel joke. First of all, it was bad enough that Charlie had lost the tent. Then to be subjected to his and his wife's unbridled desire. And now to be *swimming* in his own bed ... well, it was almost more than a man could take.

The sky opened up and the deluge descended. Lightning and thunder came together now, and the wind howled so loudly it drowned out the Martins. Thank heavens for small favors, Will thought acidly. The fire sputtered and hissed and, finally, unable to keep up with the torrential downpour, petered out. Dampness penetrated his bag, chilling him to the bone, and Will wondered if it was any dryer under the trees. Probably not, he decided, and pulling his damp bag over his wet head, fantasized about killing Charlie.

Erica knew, when the first gigantic drop of rain landed on the roof of her tent like a 747 touching down, that she was in for a rough night. The drops echoed, magnified by the tightly stretched fabric of her tent. She felt as though she were trying to sleep in the middle of a bongo festival.

And if she was miserable inside the tent, she could only begin to imagine what Will was going through out there in the elements. Shivering, she threw back the top of her bag and crawled over to the flap of her tent. Drawing it back, she peered out into the darkness and tried to make out Will's sleeping bag. Lightning flashed across the sky, illuminating a brown lump huddled by the doused fire.

Without thinking, and clad in nothing but a white cotton nightgown, Erica scrambled out of the tent and sprinted through the mud, barefoot, to where Will lay.

"Will!" she shouted, trying to make herself heard above the howling wind and roaring thunder. "Will!" she shrieked again when there was no answer. The wind ripped her words out of her mouth and flung them to the seven seas. Crouching, she shook him through his sleeping bag, and almost wept with relief when his head popped out into the weather.

"What the hell are you doing out here?" he shouted, rain running like rivers across his cheeks and into his ears. "Trying to catch your death?"

"I might just ask you the same thing!" she yelled, her hands planted firmly on her hips, her hair whipping wildly around her face.

Her flimsy excuse for a nightgown, Will saw, was now completely soaked, and plastered in a most fascinating fashion to her body. Sheer white fabric, now translucent, flapped crazily in the squall, inching steadily higher on her thighs. He tore his eyes away from the nightgown and looked up at her face. "What ... do ... you ... want?" He hollered each word slowly, hoping she could understand.

What did she want? Was he crazy? What did he think she wanted? Wasn't it obvious that she was here for a moonlight stroll?

"I want you to come inside out of the rain," she shouted, and kicked his bottom with her toe. "Hurry. I'm getting soaked."

Will struggled to sit up. "Go back to bed." He pointed at her tent. "I'll be fine."

"Will!" Her teeth were chattering so badly that her toes began to cramp. "I said get in the tent." She stomped her foot in a puddle.

Will wanted nothing more on the face of this earth than to follow her to the tent. But it was dangerous. More dangerous, perhaps, than staying out there. If he went with her, he would be tempted to take their relationship to a place it had no business going ... yet. And what would the kids think? No. He was tough. He'd stay right where he was.

"Thanks, anyway," he yelled, "But really, I'll be just fine."

"You're nuts!" she shrieked.

A bolt of lightning backlit her as she stood over him. She looked like some kind of insane drowned-rat she-devil from his worst nightmare. But he grinned at her spunk.

"This is not funny. I'm not moving until you get out of that stupid bag and come with me."

That tore it. He'd had enough aggravation for one night. She was going back to bed if he had to carry her there himself. Frantically wrestling with his bag, he rolled around on the ground and fumbled for the elusive zipper. When it defiantly hid from his frozen fingers, he tried kicking and punching his way out. When that didn't work, he struggled to his feet, wiggling, shimmying and cursing, till it fell down around his ankles. Stepping out of the soggy bag, he kicked it angrily aside and, yanking on her arm, brought his nose within an inch of hers.

"You're freezing. Get back in your tent."

"Make me."

"Don't tempt me."

"I'm not going back without you."

One deafening clap of thunder rendered them silent for a moment, and the bolt of lightning that preceded it lit up the sky, illuminating them. Erica was startled by the look of raw desire she saw reflected in Will's eyes as he stood there, staring at her like a starving man.

For a brief moment, she wondered at her sanity, knowing how dangerous spending the night with him could be. She tried to think of Emily...dear, sweet Emily, who hadn't crossed her mind all day. No, better to try something else. Because of dear, sweet Emily, she was standing in the middle of an electrical storm, arguing with a madman. She suddenly had no sympathy for dear, sweet Emily. Even homeless and penniless, she was probably much better off than Erica was at the moment.

Thankfully the decision was taken out of her hands. The blinding, hair-singeing bolt of lightning—which appeared to touch down right next to them—changed her mind.

Coincidentally, it changed Will's mind at the same time.

"You go inside," he instructed. "I'll be right behind you. I want to check on the kids."

She nodded mutely and wobbled on muddy bare feet back to her tent.

Will peeked in at the kids, and found them all oblivious to the storm that raged overhead. Surprisingly, they were dry, snug and warm, and sleeping in a tangle, like a litter of puppies.

From there he ran to the supply boxes. Lifting the water-proof tarp, he rummaged around until he found several dry towels and an extra sleeping bag. He grabbed a camp lantern, a box of matches, two cans of soda and a bag of potato chips for good measure, and then bounded through the storm to the tent.

He burst through the flap with his booty and dropped it all in the middle of the bed.

"Hang on," he whispered, "while I light the lamp." His hands shook so badly he could barely strike the match. Finally, the flame took the wick and held, and the little tent was filled with a dim, flickering light. "That's better." He sighed and set the light next to the air mattress.

"Will?" Erica's muffled voice came from somewhere inside her sleeping bag.

"Hmm?"

"What's that noise?"

Will paused, then sighed again and lifted the tent flap. "Come on, boy," he coaxed. "Stop crying. We didn't forget you."

Huck leaped into the tent, delighted to have been invited to the party. Violently shaking his smelly coat, he sprayed the entire interior before turning around three or four times and settling down in the middle of the bed with a putrid yawn.

"Oh, Huck!" Erica moaned.

Well, Will thought with a wry smile, so much for romance.

Chapter Eight

Erica pushed herself up in the sleeping bag and watched Will zip the tent flap shut. A chill, starting at her neck, moved through her body and threatened to rattle her teeth right out of her head.

"What should we do first?" she chattered, and glanced nervously around the compact space the three unlikely bedfellows now shared. The air mattress, somewhere between a twin and a double in size, was beginning to feel a little crowded. With Will taking up one end, and Huck and the pile of supplies taking up the center, Erica wondered how she'd get a wink of sleep on the two square feet left for her.

"I, ah...ah...ah..." Will sneezed noisily. "I think we should start by getting out of these wet clothes." He eyed her damp nightgown with concern.

Erica fished her pack out from under her pillow. "I brought some extra-large T-shirts. Want one?"

Considering his body was now one giant goose bump, he only hesitated for a moment over the hot-pink shirt she held out to him. It was dry. It was warm. This was no time to play macho man. He whisked the shirt out of her hand.

"That'd be great. Thanks."

Quickly stripping to his briefs, he tossed his soggy clothes into a heap in the corner and used one of the towels he'd brought with him to dry his hair. For a moment, Erica forgot the chill and watched in fascination as he rubbed his torso with the terry cloth. Her mouth went dry, and she tried to swallow. He was so incredibly beautiful. In all her years of nursing, Erica had never seen a more perfect specimen. And though her nightgown was still soaking wet, she'd suddenly stopped shivering. Her eyes darted to her hands as he finished drying himself, and she hoped that he hadn't caught her staring.

"Don't just sit there," he chided. "Get out of that wet thing and dry off."

Erica fidgeted in the flickering lamplight and knew that there was no way she could undress in front of this man. Being with him, alone like this, was far too risky. Feeling completely vulnerable, she twisted the hem of her damp gown into a knot.

"What's wrong?" He stopped drying his hair and arched a quizzical eyebrow at her.

"I, uh, could you...?" She drew a circle in the air with her finger.

"Oh..." Will smiled his lazy, off-center smile and presented his back to her.

She hastily ripped her wet gown off and dried herself with the other towel he'd brought. Pulling her large T-shirt over her head, she ran her fingers through her hair and hoped that she at least looked halfway decent.

In the dim lamplight, Will watched with interest her blunted shadow move and sway on the tent wall. It seemed suddenly warmer in their crowded quarters and he felt his blood begin to thaw and flow. When she arched her back and shook her silky mane of shiny brown hair over her shoulders, he had to look away. She was taking a real risk letting him in there to spend the night. So, obviously, she trusted him. And here he was, abusing that trust by getting all hot and bothered over a simple shadow. Maybe it was time to think about baseball again.

"I'm done," she announced.

Will looked at the hot pink I Love Aerobics T-shirt he held in his hand with dismay before stretching it on over his head.

"It's you," Erica giggled when he turned around to face her.

"Yeah, right." He grinned. Though the tag said extralarge, it fitted Will snugly at the chest, and from there hung stylishly down to the middle of his thigh. "Makes me want to jump up and aerobicize."

"I'm afraid there's not enough room in here to work up a really good sweat," Erica teased, then bit her tongue.

"Oh, I don't know about that. . . ." Will's eyes bolted to hers and quickly jerked away. "But before we do anything, what do you say we fix up this bed?" Before we *do* anything? Lord, have mercy. Why had he said that?

"Good idea."

A constant, shrill wind whistled through the tent and its rapier slice could be easily felt through the thin walls.

"Come on, old boy." Will coaxed a reluctant Huck off the mattress and settled him at the foot of the bed. "Emily, unzip your bag and we'll use it on the bottom," he instructed, and then opened the roll he'd brought with him. "We'll use this one on top."

"Okay." The minuscule amount of warmth she'd managed to generate rapidly dissipated as she unfolded her bag and spread it out flat over the mattress.

Will flipped his roll all the way open, and once it was in place, they both scrambled under its cover. Careful not to touch, they lay stiffly at opposite ends of the bed, Erica at the head and Will at the foot. Lifting his wheezy muzzle up onto the mattress and snuffling noisily, Huck found and slobbered in Will's ear.

"Get!" Will pushed the amorous Huck out of the way, and turning off the camp light, plunged them into pitch-darkness. They lay for what seemed like hours—though it was probably no more than five or ten minutes—tossing and turning, unable to get warm.

Finally, it was Huck's malodorous breath that drove Will to speak to Erica.

"Psst. Emily? Are you awake?"

Erica questioned the wisdom of answering him, feeling it was perhaps best to leave sleeping dogs lie. But curiosity got the better of her. "Yes," she whispered into the blackness. She could feel him shivering almost as violently as she was. "Why?"

"Uh...well—" he hesitated. "—I was, uh, thinking that under the circumstances, maybe it would be okay to share some body warmth. You know—" he took a deep breath and finished in a shivery rush "—before one of us expires from hypothermia."

"Oh, sure," she agreed, and scooted awkwardly to the middle of the bed. Stiffening, she felt Will crawl up beside her and slip under the cover.

"Here," she said, and moved her pillow between them. "We can share."

"Thanks," he whispered, and settled his head next to hers. She lay perfectly still, mystified as to the logistics of sharing her body warmth with Will in a platonic way. Should she lean against him? Throw her arms around him? Toss her legs over his? As she self-consciously pondered her dilemma in the dark, Will took the decision out of her hands.

"What are you doing way over there?" he asked.

His sexy voice was low in her ear. Circling her waist with his arm, he dragged her over to his side of the bed and up tight against his body, spoon fashion.

"I, uh, don't know," she gasped in surprise.

"We'll never warm up if we don't work together on this," he chastised her lightly. "Let's start by getting that blood flowing again." He vigorously rubbed her arm with his hand.

It's flowing, all right, she thought hazily. For the first time since she'd been out by the fire, Erica was beginning to warm up. Melt down. Whatever. She suddenly felt drowsy and wonderful in the curve of Will's strong, warm body.

His hand stilled and she nestled more firmly against him.

"Better?" he whispered.

"Much." She nodded happily against the muscular chest that spoke of his love for aerobics. "How 'bout you?"

"I'm heating up," he admitted.

She decided to let that go. "I can't believe the kids slept through this storm." Turning on her back, she angled her face over to Will's.

"They were exhausted." He tightened his arm around her waist and drew his knee up onto her hip.

"Umm. All that running around."

"Umm."

The wind continued to howl.

"Will?" She felt deliciously warm and comfortable.

"Hmm?" He felt more relaxed than he had in years.

"This is the strangest wind I've ever heard. It howls like a wild animal in pain."

Will was silent.

"What was that?" Erica nervously gripped the wrists that were tightly crossed at her stomach.

"Don't worry." He patted her stomach. "I'm pretty sure I know what that is, and it's nothing to be afraid of."

"It's not a wild animal?"

"Not exactly."

Her mouth hung open. "It *can't* be the Martins."

"I'm afraid so."

"You mean they're *still* at it?" She was incredulous. "Really?"

"Really."

"Isn't that rather...unusual?" she asked, and twisted onto her side to face him. "And they're so...noisy." Erica's eyes had adjusted to the dark and she could see the broad grin on Will's face. She elbowed him lightly in the ribs.

A particularly lusty howl rode the wind into the tent. Raising his head, Huck cocked his ear in the direction of the sound. As it hit its crescendo, he buried his head under his paws and whimpered. Will and Erica took one look at each other and nearly died laughing.

"Won't they wake the kids?" she asked when she could finally speak.

"Nah." Will pulled her head up onto his chest. "They're used to it. I, on the other hand, don't think I'll ever get used to that."

The sounds of love continued to ebb and flow and Will was forced to lean into his pillow and roar.

Pulling the sleeping bag up over their heads, Erica attempted to mute the laughter that shook them both.

"Shh." She placed a finger over his warm, smiling lips. "They'll be able to hear us!" she gasped in warning.

He kissed her finger. "So?" he murmured through the silky lock of hair that lay across his cheek. Picking it up, he used it to tickle her face. "We can hear them," he argued.

"Yes," she agreed, and levered herself up to hover lightly over his body. "But that's different. They're not laughing at us."

"True." Will gripped her upper arms and pulled her down, onto his massive chest. "However, I don't think we are being any more obnoxious than they are. I mean, really, it's not like they couldn't control themselves for one little weekend."

"I don't know," Erica mused. "I've never experienced...um," she stammered, embarrassed. "You know, such an overpowering, uh, physical relationship." Horrified at her candid admission, she looked down her nose into Will's eyes.

For reasons that were a mystery to him, Will was thrilled. "Me, neither," he confessed.

"Really?" she blurted out, curious. Not even with June? she wondered, as she lowered her head back down to his chest.

"Really. Not like that, anyway." Unless he counted the time he'd kissed her in the barn. He hadn't exactly bayed at the moon. But then again, he hadn't been completely in control, either. Maybe he was beginning to understand these animalistic compulsions.

Emily was like no other woman he'd ever known. She had the ability to make him feel things he never allowed himself to feel. He never felt younger or more vibrant than when he spent time in her company. Together they seemed to generate a certain power. A power that had a life of its own. Almost as though when they were together, the way they were now, they became alive. As one. And it felt so good to be alive. For so long he'd slogged through his day feeling half-dead. Incomplete.

But, Emily had changed all that for him. In the short time since she'd returned from San Francisco, he'd come to depend on her strength. Her energy. Her ability to make him laugh with a carefree abandon that he'd never experienced with another living being. Not even June, he noted with a twinge of guilt. No. The sheer exhilaration he now felt almost constantly came from Emily, and Emily alone. There never was, and could never be, a more perfect person for him than her.

Pulling her head up into the curve of his neck, he sighed. He guessed he knew he was a goner the day of that crazy haircut she'd given him. The only thing that troubled him about the way he was feeling now was, when the time came, would he be able to let her go? Did he have the strength to deal with yet another loss?

Erica shifted in his arms and listened to the comforting sound of his steady heartbeat. He'd grown suddenly quiet, and she wondered what he could be thinking as he absently stroked the hair at her nape.

"Will?" she whispered, his name barely a sigh on her lips.

Gripping the back of her neck, he pulled her face up next to his and groaned. "What?" he asked, frustration tinge-ing his voice.

"Nothing." She sighed.

Will was unable to stand the tension any longer. The crazy circumstances that had thrown them in the tent together ceased to exist. The only thing that mattered to him now was the vital, alluring woman at his side.

Rolling over, he took Erica with him and pinned her be-neath his body. She was his for now. Deciding not to worry about losing her, he instead chose to enjoy to the fullest their short time together. This might be the last time he would ever lay beside this amazing woman, and he decided to make the most of it.

"Come here," he muttered against her mouth before closing his lips over hers. He could feel her relax beneath him, as she ran her delicate hands over his shoulders and locked them at the back of his neck.

Will changed the angle of his mouth to deepen the kiss and she moaned softly, her hands exploring the thick, soft hair she found at the back of his head. She was warm and pliant, melting into him.

Though she knew that she should stop, Erica never felt more compelled to do anything in her life than to lose her-self in the magic of Will's embrace. She'd meant what she'd said earlier to Will about never having experienced an over-powering physical relationship. But now, under the circum-stances, she was beginning to rethink that statement.

She must be completely overcome with desire for Will. How else could she possibly let herself betray her sister in such a manner? She pushed the disturbing thought to the back of her mind and gave herself up to the sensations Will's kisses brought.

The abrasion of his whiskers on her soft cheek. The roughness of his hands on her arms. The perfect fit of his lips over hers. The smell, the taste, the feel that was uniquely Will Spencer. She ran her hands over the biceps that bulged like boulders in his powerful arms, over his broad, capable shoulders, his strong jaw. Running her hands alongside their mouths, she attempted to trace their kiss with her fingertips. Will drew her forefinger into his mouth and nibbled at it, breaking their kiss.

"Isn't this where we started?" he asked, nipping her fingertip. Dropping it, he settled on her lower lip and pulled it into his mouth.

"Umm." She smiled as he rolled them back onto their sides. Her breathing was as ragged as his and their hearts hammered at the same frenzied pace.

"Hey," he whispered, and she could sense his grin.

"What?"

"I feel like howling."

"Me, too." She returned his grin.

Throwing back his head, Will howled just loud enough to set Huck off.

"Uh-oh," Erica giggled as they sat up to see the aged mongrel sitting at the end of the bed, soulfully returning Will's call.

Deciding he was being asked to join his tent mates on the bed, Huck crawled on his belly between Will and Erica and whimpered appealingly.

"Who invited you?" Will asked gruffly, pushing at the ancient mutt. How was he supposed to continue sharing his body warmth with Emily, when this lifeless bag of bones lay sprawled out between them?

"Oh, never mind." Erica sympathetically stroked the mangy, wrinkled old head. "Maybe he should stay where he is," she said meaningfully, and looked over at Will. "Maybe this way we'll . . . um . . ."

"Behave ourselves?" Will supplied, and patted the dog's head for a moment before twining his fingers with hers. "You're probably right." Will sighed.

Erica nodded. She knew how he felt. She was just as frustrated as he was. But at the same time, she was tremendously relieved. They'd been close to stepping beyond the point of no return. And that was something, no matter how desperately she wanted it, she could never allow herself to do.

Huck's offensive breath finally brought Erica out of her languid dreams to the edge of wakefulness. Somehow, during the night, she must have changed places with the dog, because her back was pulled tightly against Will's chest, while Huck was nestled firmly against her stomach. Smiling drowsily, she felt like the insides of a softly snoring sandwich. Yawning contentedly, she burrowed more closely into Will's embrace and he tightened his arm possessively across her middle.

"Good morning," he mumbled in her ear, and yawned.

His breath tickled the hair on her neck and she shivered deliciously. She could get used to waking up like this. With the exception of Huck, of course, who chose that moment to yawn in her face.

"Eeeww," Erica moaned. "Don't your owners ever brush your teeth?"

"What teeth?" Will grinned and pulled his chin up onto her shoulder so he could see the dog. "He only has two or three left, and those are broken."

Knowing that he was the center of interest, Huck tiredly flopped his tail and kissed Erica on the lips.

"Ahack!" she spit, and turned toward Will to wipe her face on his shirt.

Will laughed. "I have to admit that compared with him, we smell fresh as daisies."

"Speak for yourself." Erica tried to bury her head under the covers, away from Will's probing eyes. "What do we do for a shower around here? And *please* don't say it's in the woods," she mumbled into his chest.

"No." His mirth rumbled in her ear. "You grab a bar of soap and head down to the river."

"Ugh."

Will ducked under the covers to join her. "You can't hide in here all day," he chided, and tickled her ribs.

"Oh, yes, I can." She laughed and proceeded to roll around, playfully wrestling with him under the covers.

"What are you guys doin'?"

A childish question filtered through the sleeping bag and they froze beneath its surface, midtickle.

"Uh-oh," Erica whispered.

"Busted," Will breathed. He threw back the covers, and the static electricity caused their hair to stand straight out at crazy angles. Six pairs of curious young eyes peered into the tent at them. Everyone was giggling, except Sam, who looked horrified.

"What are you doing in here, Dad?" she asked accusingly.

Will and Erica exchanged guilty glances.

"I came in here to get out of the storm last night, sweetheart," Will explained gently.

Samantha's eyes narrowed in suspicion. "What storm?"

Erica laughed at the absurdity of the situation. "You mean you kids didn't hear anything last night?"

"Like what?" Sam was a bloodhound on the trail of truth, justice and the American way.

"Like thunder and lightning and buckets of rain, that's what." Will grew weary of the interrogation. "Now, if you

don't mind, why don't you guys get out of here and give
Emily a chance to freshen up before you begin torturing her
with questions.''

The look Sam gave them, before she followed her cousins to the river, was filled with fear. Erica stared after the
young girl and her heart went out to her.

''We're in trouble now,'' she murmured.

''She'll get over it.'' Will sighed and ran a hand over the
stubble on his jaw.

''Yes, but, Will, she's scared to death that something
happened between us.'' She was suddenly very relieved that
she and Will hadn't done anything they'd regret, last night
in the turbulent storm.

''I doubt it. She's too young to put two and two together
like that.''

Erica rolled her eyes and pulled the covers back up over
her head. Chuckling, Will reached down and drew them
back, away from her face.

''Okay, okay. I'll talk to her,'' he promised, and tweaked
her nose. ''Stop worrying so much.''

''It's just that I know what she's thinking and I hate to
have her worry unnecessarily.''

Will pulled on his still-damp jeans and squinted thoughtfully at her. ''Maybe she's not worrying so unnecessarily,''
he said before scooting through the tent flap. ''See you at
the river,'' he called over his shoulder.

Erica stared after Will in surprise. What had he meant by
that? Shifting her gaze to Huck, she said, ''Come on, old
boy. Let's go get a bath. A nice ice-cold romp in the river
will keep us out of trouble, right?''

Huck favored her with a toothless grin before following
Will out of the tent and down to the river.

The breakfast dishes had all been cleared away and the
last of the camping supplies were being broken down and
packed by the adults. The kids were each assigned loads to

tote down to the river, where Will would carry them across the tree bridge and stow them in the supply raft.

"Come here." Sam gripped Rachel's arm as they trudged back to the campsite after depositing a load with Will.

"Where?" Rachel asked as her cousin pulled her off the trail and into the woods. "What are you doing?"

Sam stopped when they were hidden from view. "I want to play a trick on Emily."

Rachel looked curiously at Sam. "Why?"

"To pay her back for always bossing us around, that's why."

Rachel's young brow furrowed quizzically. "I don't think she seems bossy. I like her."

Sam blew an exasperated puff of air. "Well, you don't have to live with her the way I do, so of course you think she's nice. Anyway, it's no big deal, and it won't hurt anyone, but I need your help."

"Well, okay." Rachel shrugged. "But we'd better not get into trouble."

Erica was beginning to fear she'd become hopelessly lost. She knew it was foolish to have gone searching for Sam without telling anyone where she was going. But she had her reasons.

When Rachel told her that Sam had run away, she had the funniest feeling it was her fault the girl had run off. And not wanting to alarm the others unnecessarily, she'd decided to find her and have a talk with her before anyone was the wiser.

The only problem was, she discovered as she squinted up at the sun, trying to discern her location, she didn't have a clue where she was. Or where the campsite was, for that matter. Or where Sam was. If she could get lost this easily, where on earth was little Sam? Images of the young girl, lost and crying, perhaps even running from a bear, tortured Erica as she made her way through the forest thicket.

"Sam," she cried. Her breathing was fearful, ragged. She stopped to wipe her eyes and nose on her sleeve. "Sam, where are you, honey?" Her only answer was the occasional scolding of an angry squirrel.

"Has anyone seen Emily?" Will asked the group in general as they prepared to embark on the next leg of their journey.

"Maybe the bear got her," Danny speculated boyishly. Rachel shot Sam a look of pure terror.

"I don't like it," Will muttered. "She's been gone for over an hour now. I'm going to go look for her. You guys stay here and wait for us to get back."

Charlie hiked his pants up a notch and manfully adjusted his broken glasses. "I'll go with you, Will. She could be hurt and you might need some help bringing her back."

If she wasn't hurt, she would be by the time Charlie got through with her, Will thought. "No, Charlie, you stay here and keep an eye on everyone. Hopefully I won't be gone long."

Unable to stand the guilt of their monstrous deed for another moment, Sam and Rachel ran after Will and grabbed him by the arms.

"Dad! Dad, it's my fault that Emily is gone. Rachel told her that I ran away and I hid from her when she went out to look for me," Sam bawled, tears of real fear streaking her cheeks.

"What?" Will couldn't believe what he was hearing. Looking at the stricken girls, he knew they were telling the truth, and an icy-cold finger of dread traced his spine. If anything happened to her, he didn't know what he would do.

Red-hot fury raged in his eyes as he gazed at the two contrite girls at his side. Sam met his gaze and dropped his arm. Her expression was awestruck, as though she'd never seen her father so mad before.

"I'll deal with you two later," he told them, a muscle in his jaw jumping angrily. He strode purposefully over to the supply raft and picked up his rifle.

Sam and Rachel screamed in horror.

"I'll *talk* to you two later," he clarified grimly before striding off into the woods.

Erica sat on a fallen log and desperately tried to get her bearings. On which side of the tree did the moss grow? The north side? And if that was true, what should she do with this information? Walk north? Why? What was north? Just more trees, she reckoned futilely, and lifted her damp hair off the back of her neck and fanned herself with her hand.

She wanted to just sit and cry for a while, but realizing that that would get her nowhere in a big hurry, decided to continue her hunt for Sam. Poor Sam, she thought, her throat closing painfully at the thought of her little girl lost in the woods. Swallowing past the lump in her throat, she wished she'd thought to bring some water. It was hot. And she was tired, sticky and frantic with worry.

As she stood to resume her search she could hear the sounds of some very large, very mysterious creature crashing down the hillside toward her. It was far too large to be Sam, and the only thing Erica imagined it could be was her bear. Back this time to polish her off. Kicking into high gear, Erica plunged through the underbrush, down the hillside, away from the animal in hot pursuit.

At least he's chasing me and not little Sam was Erica's last conscious thought before she ran right into a low-lying branch.

Chapter Nine

Where was she running so fast? Will wondered, sprinting down the hill, trying for all he was worth to catch Emily. He was going to have a heart attack. Hell, he was moving so fast and breathing so hard, he couldn't even call her name. She disappeared from sight and Will paused for a moment to take in some much-needed oxygen before plunging into the woods after her.

Just as he thought his heart couldn't possibly pump any faster, his eyes lit on a flash of color lying at the base of a tall pine tree. Emily. She must have fallen. Please...let her be all right, he pleaded, wrestling berry vines and low branches as he made his way to her side.

"Emily!"

Her face was streaked with tears and dirt. She was scratched and scraped, bloodied and bruised, red-faced and sweaty, and she never looked more beautiful to him than she did right then. Will could have sworn he felt his heart physically swell with love for her at that moment. Getting down next to her on one knee, he cradled her head in his hands.

"Sweetheart? It's me, Will. Can you hear me?" He pulled a blade of grass out of her hair and searched her face for some sign of life. Her eyes fluttered as she tried to open them.

"Honey, are you all right?"

"Umm," she moaned, and focused on him. Grimacing, she attempted to smile. "I think I knocked the wind out of myself." Her laugh was weak.

"How?"

Will's handsome face was etched with concern, she saw. He smoothed her hair out of her face clumsily, tenderly, with his large hands.

Pointing at the branch she'd so unceremoniously ricocheted off only moments before, she whispered hoarsely, "I thought I was running from a bear and I bounced off that."

"Where did it hit you?"

"Here." She pointed high on her stomach, just under her ribs.

Without waiting for her permission, Will pulled her light cotton blouse from the waistband of her pants and lifted it high, up onto her breasts. A bright red slash ran across her smooth, flawless flesh, turning purple in some spots already. He probed her rib cage with his fingertips and ran his hands over her abdomen, gently pushing and prodding, searching for some sign of serious injury.

"Take a deep breath," he ordered, and when she complied, he watched her face. "Did that hurt?"

"I don't think I have any broken ribs, if that's what you're asking," she replied, looking down as his hands became acquainted with her waistline. She marveled at how such work-roughened hands could be so gentle. Reaching up, she rested her hands lightly on top of his, tracing his movements with her fingertips. "Really, I'm going to be fine."

"Don't tell me." he muttered sarcastically, "Someone ran into a tree on 'General Hospital.'"

"Will," she gasped, struggling against the pain in her
midsection. Wincing, she reached for his arm and attempted to pull herself upright, as she'd suddenly remembered the main purpose of her hunting expedition. "It's
Sam." With Will's help, she was finally able to drag herself
up to a seated position. "Sam's lost." Her voice was still
hoarse. "Hurry. We have to go find her. Rachel told me she
ran away, and I know it's all my fault," she babbled,
clutching his shirt in alarm.

Will's jaw tensed. "Honey, calm down. Sam is not lost.
She and Rachel are back at camp, safe and sound."

"Are you sure?" Her eyes flashed back and forth as she
searched his brooding expression. "What's wrong? Did
something happen to her, Will? Tell me," she demanded,
nearly frantic with worry.

"Emily, she...didn't run away at all. She and Rachel were
playing a trick on you."

Erica's lips parted and her face mirrored the hurt the girls
had inflicted. She stared at Will in shock. "They were playing a trick?" she asked, her voice thready with emotion.
"But why?"

"I don't know. Sometimes kids do dumb things." He
shook his head angrily and rubbed the tense muscles in the
back of his neck.

"I can't believe she would do something like that, Will."
Erica was beginning to share in his anger. "Does she have
any idea what she put me through? I was out of my mind
with worry." Her lower lip began to tremble. "Will, I just
don't know where I've gone wrong. She resents me. She
thinks I want to take her mother's place, and *I don't!* I want
for us to have our own relationship. And I know she thinks
something happened between us last night, and that probably scared her, but how do I tell her that nothing happened?" she rambled, trying to make him understand.

"Shh...shh." Will gathered her into his arms and rocked
her gently back and forth, as the tears one by one rolled

slowly down her cheeks. "Oh, honey." He sighed and rubbed his cheek on her forehead. "First of all, Sam loves you. She may not want to admit it yet, but she loves you." Will rested his chin on the top of her head. He knew just how Sam felt. Sometimes new feelings were hard to recognize, let alone admit. "And second, as far as I'm concerned, something did happen between us last night." He tipped her chin up, and his eyes held hers. "Something special."

"Really?" she whispered, before he lowered his mouth to hers for the softest, gentlest, most exquisite kiss Erica had ever experienced. How could a man so large, so masculine, so rough around the edges at times kiss her with such amazing tenderness, she wondered hazily, as she twisted in his embrace in order to pull herself closer. She gave herself up to his touch, momentarily forgetting her pain, both physical and emotional. Will said something special was happening, she thought in exultation. And so it was. She'd figure out what to do about it later.

Breathing heavily, Will finally released her mouth and shook his head. "We'd better stop, or we might never make it back to camp." He squeezed her arms and playfully kissed the tip of her nose. "Besides, I have to go give a couple of brats a piece of my mind."

"Oh, Will, don't," Erica pleaded. After she'd had a moment to adjust to the fact that she'd been the victim of a childish prank, it didn't seem quite so painful after all. Erica was pretty sure that the girl had acted out of fear, not malice.

Will looked at her and smiled grimly. "We'll see" was all he would say, as he helped her slowly to her feet.

As they walked back toward camp in silence, Will thought about what could have happened if he hadn't been fortunate enough to spot Emily tearing down the hillside. His heart lurched fearfully as unwanted, morbid possibilities tortured his imagination with vivid clarity. He was pretty

darn lucky that everything had turned out all right this time.
Last time he'd lost someone he'd loved—

He snapped out of his woolgathering with the shocking,
yet heady realization that he'd fallen in love. Again. This
time, harder than ever before.

And as he walked along beside the woman he now knew
he loved more than life itself, he had the strangest and most
wonderful feeling that sweet, angelic June was smiling at
him from somewhere up above.

When Will finally returned to camp with Erica safely by
his side, she was immediately engulfed in a relieved and
tearful two-family hug. Sam clung to her longer and more
tightly than anyone else.

"Oh, Emily. I'm so sorry." Sam buried her head in Erica's chest. "I didn't know you'd get lost, honest. I was just
being a brat." She looked up into Erica's face, her light blue
eyes filled with tears of regret. "Do you forgive me?"

Erica hugged her hard and kissed the top of the young
girl's head. "Of course I forgive you, sweetheart." She
caught Will's eyes as she held his daughter in her arms and
they smiled at each other.

"We thought maybe a bear decided to chase you again,"
Danny piped up when the dust had settled. "Or maybe eat
you."

"Danny." Will shot his son a warning glance, and the boy
blushed and hung his head.

"Sorry," he mumbled.

Erica grinned at him and patted Sam on the back. "Nope,
no bears this time. Although I thought I caught a glimpse of
Bigfoot out there."

"Really?" The children all gathered around her in awe.

"Yes, but then I realized it was just Will coming to save
me," she teased the openmouthed kids.

"Come on, you guys." Will pointed impatiently at the
rafts. "Let's get this show on the road. We've wasted

enough time today already. If we're going to make it to the next site before dark, we'd better hustle.''

It took a while for everyone to gear up to the raucous, carefree feeling of the day before. But by the time the group had finally arrived at the midway point and stopped for some lunch, everyone was feeling lighthearted and relaxed. The rafts were pulled up onto the shore far enough so that they wouldn't be washed away, and only enough supplies were unpacked to make a lunch of sandwiches, chips and soda pop. Everyone sat in a loose circle, on whatever fallen log or rock made a decent seat, and laughed and joked, filled with the spirit of high adventure. Everyone, that is, except Sam, who sat off by herself on a tree stump near the river's edge.

"Hi. Mind if I join you?" Erica stood, paper plate and cup in hand, looking down at the reflective teen.

Sam smiled bashfully and nodded.

"You're kind of quiet. Is everything all right?"

"I guess."

Erica studied the child's pensive expression. "Would you like to talk about it?" she asked gently, sensing that something much deeper lay behind her quiet demeanor.

"I guess."

Erica wished again for the umpteenth time that she had Emily's way with children. Emily always knew the perfect thing to say in any circumstance. She could talk the birds out of the trees. All Erica seemed to be able to elicit from the normally chatty teen was a halfhearted "I guess." It was so frustrating. Because she didn't know what else to do, she remained silent and bit into her peanut butter sandwich.

Her silent acceptance was all Sam seemed to need.

"You know, last time we did this...you know, camping...my mom was here." Sam looked tentatively at Erica for her reaction.

Busy with the peanut butter, Erica tried to wrestle her tongue free from the roof of her mouth in order to respond. Before she could organize her oral capabilities, Sam forged ahead.

"Sometimes I miss her so much." Sam's eyes glazed over with a faraway look. "She used to love camping with us. She used to make this really horrible campfire stew. That's what she called it. It would have everything that was left from the supply box in it. You know, hot dogs, chili, corn chips, pickles, hamburger.... And I hated it. She would make us eat it." Sam glanced up at Erica. "Kind of like you."

Having just filled her mouth with another load of peanut butter, Erica could only nod dumbly. Taking this as a sign to continue, Sam treated Erica to a rare glimpse of June the wife and mother. She reminisced about camping trips past and other vacations, and shared memories of special holidays and occasions in the Spencers' lives. June must have been a wonderful woman, Erica mused sadly, and wondered how anyone could ever live up to the standards she'd set.

Curious, Will finished his sandwich and ambled, unnoticed by the noisy lunch crowd, over to where Erica and Sam sat deep in conversation. He stood out of their line of vision, knowing he was eavesdropping, yet unable to stop himself. As he settled against the trunk of a massive old redwood, his daughter's youthful voice reached his ears, and he was suddenly transported back in time. Her vivid memories surprised him as she painted a colorful picture of his life with June, then gently led him back to the here and now. Back to the reality of their lives today.

"Even though she died more than two years ago, I still miss her so much it hurts sometimes. I'm a lot better now, but I wish she were here." Taking a deep breath, she turned to Erica. "But you know what really scares me?"

Erica shook her head.

"Sometimes I can't remember some stuff about her. Sometimes I even forget what she looked like and I get scared." A large tear squeezed its way past her long, dark lashes, and Erica instinctively gathered the girl into her arms. "And I feel really guilty, because I can't remember," she sniffed, her young shoulders sagging with a burden far too heavy for a child. "And sometimes I even wish for a new mom. You know, someone to talk to about girl stuff. I know I should just go to Dad, but he just doesn't get it." She swiped at her cheeks with an angry fist.

Will tried to swallow past the painful lump that had lodged in his throat as he watched Emily run her hands through his daughter's midnight black hair. Hair that was the exact shade June's had been. She murmured comforting words to the child, and Will could feel himself falling more deeply—if that was possible—in love.

"Oh, honey. You can't feel guilty about wanting a mother. Why that's the most natural thing in the world. Everybody needs a mother from time to time. Even the president of the country. I still need to talk to my mom about girl stuff."

"Really?" Sam peered up at Erica in surprise.

"Sure. All the time."

"So you don't think I'm a real loser for wanting a mom?"

"Of course not. Sam, honey, you had a wonderful mother. From what you tell me, she sounds like the best. I'm sure I would have liked her very much. Nothing can ever take away from her love for you. Or your love for her."

"Yeah?"

"Yeah."

Sam sent her a watery grin. "Sometimes I wish you were my new mom. Even if you do make us eat veggies all the time."

Sam's innocent words filled Erica with great joy and sadness at the same time. As she squeezed Sam around the shoulders, her laughter was poignant.

"Well, yes, but you have to admit, the veggies have done wonders for your figure. You're positively skinny these days." It was true. Sam had lost at least ten pounds since the day Erica had arrived from San Francisco.

Blushing, Sam cast her eyes down into her lap and, without looking up, said, "Em, can I ask you a question?"

"Sure, honey. Anything."

"How come my dad slept with you last night?"

Erica froze for a moment, taken off guard by the child's pointed question.

Will leaned forward off the tree and grinned, straining to hear her response.

"Sam, didn't any of you kids hear the thunder and lightning last night?"

The girl shook her head blankly.

"Well, do you remember the thunder during your dad's story about the bear last night? All you kids screamed because at first you thought it could be a bear?"

"I didn't think it, but yeah, I remember." She nodded.

"Well, sometime after we all went to bed, the thunder got worse. There was lightning, too, and then rain. Lots of rain. Your poor dad was lying out there in the downpour with Huck and they were both getting soaked. It looked like they were trying to sleep in the shower."

Sam giggled.

"When the wind started to blow, it got cold out there, and since I was the only person with extra space in my tent, I went out to get your dad and Huck. At first he didn't want to come inside, but when a bolt of lightning almost cooked the two of us, he changed his mind."

"Oh."

"Sam?" Erica tipped the girl's still-downcast face up with a gentle finger. "Even though your father's love life is his own business, I want you to know that your father and I didn't...well, that is, there wasn't any, um, I guess what I'm trying to say is nothing happened last night."

Will's grin broadened. Good job, he thought, amused at her discomfort with the topic of conversation.

"Oh." Sam glanced shyly down at her hands and back up at Erica. "Em, do you love my dad?"

Heart pounding, Will clung to the tree and strained to hear her answer.

This kid doesn't pull any punches, Erica thought, once again taken aback by the child's frank question. As of yet, Will had said nothing about loving her, but unfortunately for everyone involved, Erica was afraid she'd fallen head over heels in love with Will the moment he'd caught her staring at his house that first day on the job.

"Honey, at this point in time, that's between your father and me. But I can tell you this. If I could pick a little girl and boy to be my very own, and if I could pick a man to be their father and my husband, well, I would be delighted to choose you guys. I love you all as though you were my own family."

His heart thrumming wildly in his ears, Will came to the conclusion that it was only a matter of time before they all became a family. It was then he knew beyond a shadow of a doubt that he would remarry. And the woman he would ask to marry him would be Emily. It still amazed him that for the first two and a half months she had worked for him, he hadn't really even noticed her. Why had it taken him so long to wake up and see what a jewel she was? Thank heavens he finally had. She was everything he could ever want in a wife and mother, and more.

Erica tugged on one of Samantha's raven locks. "I want you to know that no matter what happens between your dad and me, I will always love you and Danny. I couldn't love you any more if I really were your mother."

Blinking rapidly, Sam beamed up at Erica. "I love you, too, Em," she said bashfully, and snuggled more tightly into her arms.

Em. Emily should be here holding this child, Erica
thought guiltily. In a fit of maternal instinct, she'd taken her
relationship with Will's children even further into the forbidden, leaving her more ashamed than ever before. What
had she done now?

Eyes blurry, Will pushed off the tree and walked back to
the raucous lunch group, who were beginning to clean up
after their meal. June would have approved of this woman,
he thought, overcome by sweet, poignant emotions he
couldn't keep at bay. For some reason, that was important
to him. Just as important as it was that July like her. And
she did. He could tell. Smiling to himself, Will brushed at
his eyes with his fingers. Thanks to Emily, everything would
finally be all right.

"Let's go, everybody," he shouted, and picking up a box
of lunch supplies, herded an excited gaggle of kids and a
rock-eating mutt down to the river.

The next campsite was far less perilous than the first, at
least as far as the river was concerned. A large, very deep,
slowly moving area near their landing point made what the
kids considered to be the perfect swimming hole. Someone
from an earlier camping trip had tied a long, thickly knot-
ted rope high in the branches of an old fir tree, and the kids
amused themselves by swinging out over the water and
plunging into its sparkling blue depths. Unable to resist the
squeals of delight, the adults abandoned their efforts at setting up camp and opted to join the kids for a refreshing dip.

It was hot and Erica was anxious to wash her hair. Grabbing a bottle of shampoo from her backpack, she stripped
out of her khaki shorts and top, down to her brightly col-
ored bikini, and headed to the river to accomplish her task.
Which, as it turned out, was not as easy as she'd envi-
sioned.

"Need some help?" Will asked over her shoulder as she
lunged for the shampoo bottle that bobbed just beyond her

grasp. "Here," he said, and reaching around her, scooped the bottle out of the water. "Didn't you tell me once that you liked having someone else do your hair?"

She couldn't believe he actually remembered that. "Um-hmm." She nodded, brushing the water out of her eyes with the backs of her hands. He was standing waist-deep in the water, next to her, his wet hair pushed appealingly off his face. A boyish grin stole crookedly across his mouth as he boldly appreciated the way her damp suit clung to her curves. Feeling herself growing warm under his probing stare, she glanced pointedly at the bottle he still held in his hand. "Are you volunteering for the job?"

"Yep." He lifted an insolent lip and took a step toward her. Pulling her into his arms, he drew her back and dipped her hair into the water, taking care not to submerge her face. He ran his hands slowly through her hair, until he was satisfied that it was completely wet, then brought her back to her feet.

"You're sure this is shampoo and not Nair or something," he teased. "I wouldn't want to give you a bald spot by mistake."

She rolled her eyes at his charming grin. "I'm sure."

Standing over her from behind, he poured the shampoo into the palm of his hand and gently massaged it into her hair.

Erica closed her eyes and gave herself up to the sensations of Will's hands sliding sensuously through the lather. How would she ever be able to explain any of this to Emily? she wondered hazily. Obviously she would find out about everything. Will would no doubt remind her of many details after they were married. How would Emily react? Her heart skipped a beat at the thought of her sister married to Will. She moaned. Partly from her guilty conscience and partly from the exquisite pleasure Will was bringing her.

"Feel good?" His voice was a low whisper in her ear.

"Umm." She nodded, unable to speak.

"Hang on," he directed, and slowly lowered her back into the water, where he rinsed her hair so thoroughly it squeaked. "There you go. All done."

"Thanks," she murmured, still holding on to his upper arms for support. As they stood smiling at each other, Erica once again forgot why she was feeling so guilty.

"Ow!" Danny's eyes blazed angrily at his sister. "Stop hitting me!"

"You had a mosquito on your cheek." She could feel Erica's quelling stare and meekly defended her aggressive behavior.

"I don't care. Next time you hit me I'm going to clean your clock," he declared grumpily.

Tempers were flaring. Not only had the humidity reached an almost unbearable level, the already thick air was even thicker with mosquitoes. Like kamikaze pilots on missions of death, they plagued the entire group with nasty, itchy welts. Everyone sat slapping themselves and one another in a futile attempt to lessen the insect population.

Charlie did his best to wage war on the annoying critters with a fly swatter, but soon discovered that the only thing he was unable to destroy were the mosquitoes. After knocking over the card table that contained the dirty dinner dishes and a large pail of soapy water, July relieved her helpful husband of his weapon and sent him off with a kiss to wait for her in the tent.

Since they were all so miserable, the time spent storytelling around the campfire was cut short, and they all decided that if they were going to be plagued, they'd rather be unconscious while it was happening. The kids turned in without complaint, again exhausted after another wild day in the woods.

Will's sleeping bag and pillow had dried out nicely in the afternoon sun, so he rolled it out by the fire and prepared to turn in, too. Once again, he and Erica were the last two up

Erica watched him getting ready for bed and wondered how he would fare out there by the fire. As though she were reliving last night, she debated whether or not to invite him into her tent. On the one hand, she knew it would be even more dangerous than it had been the previous night, as they'd both admitted that something had happened between them. On the other hand, she couldn't let him get eaten alive by these fiendish bloodsuckers, either.

"Will?" She stepped cautiously toward the fire.

He stopped what he was doing and looked up at her with a smile. "Hmm?"

"I was just wondering how much blood you'd have left in the morning...." She grinned.

His brow furrowed as though he were deep in thought. "Hard to say," he replied, slapping at his neck. "I'm about a quart low already."

Erica giggled girlishly. "Well, I couldn't go to bed, without offering you your tent."

"Will you be in there, too?" He gripped her wrist and pulled himself up next to her.

"Um...well..." she stammered, wondering how to reply.

One look at her panicky expression, and he knew the answer. As much as he'd love a repeat performance of waking up with her nestled firmly in his arms, he knew the answer. Considering the way he felt about her now, he just couldn't risk it. This was neither the time nor the place for what he had in mind for them. When that time came, he wanted it to be magical. Holy. Not some bloody bug-slapping fest from hell, with a stinky dog and a randy pair in the tent next door.

"Ah, sweetheart. As tempted as I am, I think it would be best if I stayed out here." He gave her a quick, hard kiss on the mouth and slapped her lightly on the bottom. "Now get. Before I change my mind."

* * *

Erica couldn't decide if it was the endless drone of the mosquitoes that was driving her crazy or knowing that Will was lying somewhere just outside her tent. In any event, she was slowly being driven out of her mind. She almost wished he had taken her up on her offer. At least he could make her laugh and forget her misery.

With a sigh, she punched her pillow. That was the whole problem. Will's ability to make her forget. When she was with him she had a hard time remembering her own name, let alone her sister's.

It was incredibly hot. Maybe that's what was driving her crazy. Throwing back the top of her sleeping bag, she gave in to an impulse and snatched a towel out of her pack. She would sneak down to the river for a quick dip and be back before anyone even thought to lecture her about the dangers involved.

Clad in nothing but an extralarge T-shirt and a pair of sandals, she poked her head out of her tent and looked both ways. Huck peered up at her from where he lay next to Will and whimpered, his tail thudding once in greeting. Erica held her finger up to her lips, silently pleading with him not to give her away.

The coast seemed clear, so she seized the opportunity and slipped out of her tent and down the moonlit path that led to the river. Huck was not the only one who'd noticed her departure.

"No, boy," Will ordered the ancient hound as he pulled on a pair of softly faded blue jeans. "You stay here and guard the kids. I'll go look after her."

Huck licked Will's hand, seemingly grateful that his job required no energy on his part.

When Erica reached the swimming area, she pulled her T-shirt up over her head, kicked off her sandals and ran, buck naked, into the water. It felt wonderful to skinny-dip.

So liberating. She hadn't indulged since she was a kid. Which wasn't surprising, as there weren't that many places in San Francisco where one could run around without a stitch of clothing on.

Flipping over, she backstroked from one spot to another, cavorting and diving under the water from time to time like a porpoise.

When Erica had shed her clothes to reveal a perfectly naked silhouette, Will thought he'd have a massive coronary and drop dead on the spot. He'd really had no idea that this was what she was up to. Even though he couldn't really see a thing, just knowing that she was there a few feet away, completely and totally naked, did bad things to his blood pressure. Like a fly caught in a spider web, he was unable to move. He knew that he shouldn't stand there, watching her do something so very private, but he just couldn't tear his eyes away. Besides, what if she started to drown? he rationalized as he sat down and tried to catch his breath. It had definitely been way too long. She was magnificent. What he could see of her there in the moonlight, anyway...

Erica swam leisurely back to the shore, and thought briefly about going back to wake Will up. The night was perfect for skinny-dipping and the water felt so fine against her bare skin. Wading to the shore, she stood for a moment, backlit by the moon, and shook the water from her hair. Gathering her T-shirt off the ground, she pulled it over her head and lifted her arms so that the soft folds fell easily down over her curves.

Will watched, fascinated by what he imagined she must look like, as she stood there in silhouette. Standing, he moved silently to the center of the path, where he waited for her.

Before Erica even saw him there, bathed in the moonlight's iridescent glow, she sensed his presence. As she drew nearer, she could feel him watching her, and wondered how much he'd seen. Catching the haunted look reflected in his eyes, she froze. They stood for what seemed like an eternity, each wondering what to do next. Slowly, as though completely mesmerized, they were pulled toward each other.

"I was, uh...worried about you," he rasped, his throat incredibly dry.

"I was hot." Her statement was simple, but it impacted him like a ton of bricks.

"Me, too."

They stood, reading the double meaning in each other's eyes, and slowly going crazy. Hearts raged beneath each breastbone.

"You shouldn't go out alone at night," he said, his breathing ragged. "It's not safe."

"Why?" she whispered slowly. "Because I might meet up with a wild animal?"

The suggestion in her words pushed him over the edge, and he grabbed her and pulled her roughly up against his body and held her captive beneath his mouth. Their kiss was as fevered as the sweltering summer night. There was nothing polite or tender in this kiss, only the frenzied passion that had been building for weeks.

Gasping, searching, touching, they struggled in each other's arms, trying to satiate a hunger so voracious, it threatened to consume them both. Will backed her roughly up against a tree and settled his body into hers, desperately trying to rediscover his sanity. Would he find it in her kiss? He only knew that keeping his hands off her was destroying what was left of it.

As their kiss raged out of control, hotter and hotter until it was completely unbearable for Will both physically and emotionally, he knew they'd crossed the point of no return and that he had to make some kind of move or die.

Tearing himself away from her heavenly embrace, he

backed up, his eyes wild with desire. *Now,* a tiny voice in the back of his conscience screamed. *Now, before it's too late.*

Erica stood and watched in dumbfounded amazement as Will turned around and, without looking back, walked straight into the river.

Chapter Ten

The car tires hummed along the highway as Erica and Will sped toward St. John's. Once again, Sam and Danny had opted to ride with their cousins. This time they took Huck with them, leaving Will and Erica alone to enjoy each other's company in peace.

The rest of the raft trip had gone off without a hitch. And the day following their stay at Mosquito Coast—as Will had taken to calling it—they'd floated to their final destination and picked up the vehicles as planned by the shuttle service. Now, at last, they were on their way home.

Erica stretched like a contented cat in the warm sunlight that filled the front seat of Will's car. It was great to go away, but it was even better to go home. Home. That was how she'd come to think of Will's rambling old farmhouse.

"Penny for your thoughts." Will reached over and patted her knee with a smile. She'd been deep in thought for miles.

Playfully arching an eyebrow, she said, "I don't know...I might go crazy with such a windfall."

"Okay," he said good-naturedly. "Give me your two cents' worth."

Sitting up, Erica ran her fingers through her silky hair. "I was just thinking how nice this car smells when Huck is in the Martins' van."

Will laughed.

Her smile was melancholy. She'd miss his laugh so much. "No, really I was thinking how great it's going to be to get home. To sleep in a real bed and take a shower with real hot water and dry my hair with real electricity...wow."

"Do you mean to tell me that you found the provided accommodations less than palatial?"

Oh, and how she'd miss that crooked lift to his upper lip. "Don't get me wrong. I had a wonderful time." Will's eyes darted to hers, and the message she read there set off a fireworks display in her stomach. He had obviously had a wonderful time, as well.

Drumming his fingers on the steering wheel, Will turned back to stare at the road. He seemed nearly shy as he started to speak.

"I want to thank you for coming with us on this trip. I know it meant a lot to the kids."

"I should be the one thanking you. Really. I haven't had so much fun in a long time." And once she returned to San Francisco, she was sure she would never enjoy life again.

"Well, good." He glanced quickly at her, then back out the windshield. "It meant a lot to me...that you came with us, too." He was wound as tightly as a spring; his hands opened and closed nervously on the wheel.

"Thanks," she whispered.

"You really have a way with my kids."

Sensing that he was trying to tell her something, Erica waited expectantly for him to finish.

"They've both sort of fallen in love with you."

Her cheeks grew warm at his sweet words.

"Kind of like me."

She froze. Was he saying what she thought he was saying? Oh, my. Oh, no. Not yet. This was too soon. He wasn't supposed to land in the boat till her sister got back. Erica was horrified and thrilled to the core at the same time.

Will glanced over at her for a moment, and his eyes locked with hers. "I'm afraid that I've sort of fallen in love with you, too."

Grinning crookedly, he picked up her hand and kissed it, once again driving all rational thought right out of her head.

Will loved her! She knew his words should come as no surprise, but she was completely thunderstruck nonetheless. Her mind began to reel with questions. What would Emily say? Would she be proud that her sister had done such an effective job of landing her a man?

On the other hand, what about her? How could she give Will up now? Unlike her soft-touch sister, this was the first time in Erica's life that she'd ever fallen in love. And...she'd fallen hard.

As much as she wanted to deny Will's words, to deny what was happening, she couldn't. She was completely and totally overcome by emotion, and before she could stop the words from coming, she heard herself say, "I love you, too, Will." Mortified, she realized it was too late to retract her words. The deed had been done.

The strain in Will's face suddenly eased and he sat up a little straighter and smiled the smile of a proud and happy man in love.

Erica weakly returned his smile and wondered what would happen when everything hit the fan, as it most certainly would. Eventually Will would discover that she was not Emily. And when that happened, Erica had the depressing feeling it would be over for them all. It wasn't as if she hadn't warned Emily, she thought, angry with her scatterbrained sister. She sighed dejectedly, knowing she had a date with a broken heart in the very near future, and that knowledge took the edge off the sheer joy of finding out that Will, and his children, loved her.

Will glanced over at her, noticing the conflicting emotions at war on her pretty face. He knew it was a huge admission for them both, and he didn't want to push her. Will was pretty sure that Emily didn't take love lightly.

"Maybe," he began tentatively, "after we've had some time to adjust to the idea, we could go out to dinner and..." He ran a hand across his jaw and scratched his chin. "Figure out where to go from here."

Erica cleared her throat and tried to swallow. "Yes," she squeaked. She tried again. "Ahem... Yes, after we've all had some time to adjust, that would probably be a good idea." Time. Just how much time would it take to convince Will that even though she'd been lying through her teeth to him from the moment they'd met, she truly loved him and the kids... and could be trusted?

Probably not anytime before hell froze over, she thought miserably, and only hoped that the smile she'd fixed on her face was convincing.

While the last of the Martins' camping gear was being unloaded from the Spencers' travel trailer, July and Erica sat alone and undisturbed in the kitchen, sharing a last cup of coffee. The Spencers would be leaving for Harvest Valley shortly in order to make it home by nightfall.

July contemplated her new friend's pensive expression over the rim of her coffee cup. Taking a deep breath, she set her cup down and rested her hand lightly on Erica's arm.

"When are you going to tell him?" she asked gently, stirring Erica out of her reverie.

"I'm sorry." Erica shook her head slightly and focused on Will's sister-in-law. "I was off in la-la-land. What did you say?"

July nodded out the window at the object of Erica's trancelike gaze. Will was helping Charlie sort out their gear, as the kids chased one another energetically around the yard. "I just wondered when you were going to tell him."

"Tell him what?"

"That you are not Emily."

Rigid with shock, Erica was completely speechless.

"So, I'm right." July smiled sympathetically.

"How did you know?" Erica whispered, white as a sheet.

July looked up at the ceiling and shrugged expressively. "You're two completely different people. Anyone who has spent any amount of time with either of you could tell."

"What about Will?"

"I hate to say this, honey, and please—" July squeezed Erica's hand "—please, don't take this the wrong way, but I don't think Will really even knew your sister was alive. She just isn't his type."

Erica shook her head in disbelief. "But the kids..."

"The kids are just kids. What do they know? Besides, as far as I could tell, your sister let them spend all their time glued to the TV and phone." July shook her head. "No wonder they didn't notice. So tell me... just what is your name, anyway?"

"Erica," she replied, and returned July's grin.

"So... Erica... tell me, why did you do it?"

"It's a long story." Erica sighed and did her best to fill July in on the ridiculous escapade, while the tiny, raven-haired woman listened intently.

July blew thoughtfully on her coffee. "You're going to have to tell him, you know. He's in love with you."

Erica nodded miserably.

"And you love him, too." It was a statement of fact.

Tears brimming in her eyes, Erica nodded again.

"But you feel guilty."

Another nod. One large tear rolled down Erica's cheek and splashed in her coffee.

"Well, the way I see it," July said decisively, "if your sister really loved Will, the way she claimed to, she never would have left."

Opening her eyes, Erica stared at July. She'd never thought of it that way. But that still didn't excuse her part in the deception.

"What do you think I should do?"

"Talk to him. Explain what happened, the way you did to me. He'll understand. He's a wonderful man."

"I can't. Not until I find Emily and tell her first. She deserves that much at least."

July shrugged. "Well, in that case, I advise prayer. Lots of prayer. You'll need it." She grinned. "Erica, I don't know why, but I get the funniest feeling that you and Will are a match made in heaven."

"What smells so heavenly?" Will nuzzled the back of Erica's neck and stole the cookie off her spatula. "Mmm," he said appreciatively, biting into the chocolate-chip cookie with gusto. "I can't tell which smells better," he muttered into her ear. "You or these cookies." He buried his nose in her hair and inhaled deeply. "You," he decided. "Definitely you."

Erica turned and whacked him playfully on the backside with her spatula. "What are you doing back so early?"

"I finished up sooner than I'd expected today, and decided to come home and see what my favorite nanny was up to. Thanks for baking cookies," he mumbled enthusiastically, stuffing another one into his mouth.

"Thank Sam. She made them. I'm just taking them out of the oven for her."

Will ambled over to the refrigerator and poured himself a glass of milk. "Where is she?"

"Upstairs looking for a picture she wants to show me."

"And Danny?"

"Over at Mrs. Sealy's, picking up some books." She had all the answers now, and could barely remember the time when she hadn't known everything about this family.

Having finished his milk, Will grabbed Erica around the waist and growled in her ear. "Does this mean we're alone?"

"Till Sam comes downstairs, anyway," she said with a laugh, as Will rained a trail of kisses down her neck.

It had been like this every day in the two weeks since they'd returned. They were the picture of domestic tranquillity. And the longer Emily stayed away, the deeper Erica's feelings for Will and his children grew.

After they'd unpacked from the camping trip, the four had easily settled into the comfortable routines of a nuclear family, with Erica playing the role of Mrs. Mom to a tee. It was a role she enjoyed immensely—much to her surprise. At least, whenever she could shut out the nagging voice in the back of her mind that begged her to come clean with Will and the kids.

The only problem was, Emily still had not called. And until she did, Erica's hands were tied. The fact that Emily was still missing in action only added to Erica's stress level. She was beginning to worry about her thrill-seeking sister in earnest. Summer would be ending soon, and she was supposed to be here by now to take over. Instead she was out pretending to be homeless for a school project. She could get herself killed . . . if she hadn't already.

Erica shivered in Will's embrace. What in heaven's name was she going to do? As much as part of her wanted the charade to drag on forever, she knew it had to end. And once Will found out about the deception, he would probably never speak to her again. Or Emily.

Ignoring her father's enthusiastic display of affection on her nanny's neck, Sam burst into the kitchen and waved her scrapbook under Erica's nose.

"I found it, Em!" she exclaimed, breathless after her hasty search. Dropping the book onto the kitchen table, she plopped into a chair and flipped to the picture she was looking for. "There. See? I told you I was a blimp."

Will and Erica moved to the table to stand over her shoulder.

"You weren't a blimp, sweetheart," Will chided his daughter, and lovingly squeezed her arm. "Pleasantly plump, maybe, but not a blimp."

Sam snorted. "Dad, get real. I was a Sherman tank."

Erica laughed and pulled a fresh envelope of photos she'd taken of the kids last week off the kitchen counter. She held the new one of Sam next to the older photo in the scrapbook and whistled. "Wow, honey, you're looking good!"

"They won't believe it at school this year," she chortled, and looked up at Erica with adoration in her eyes.

Impulsively hugging the girl around her shoulders, Erica kissed her on her cheek. "I'm so proud of you," she whispered, and Sam beamed with happiness.

The back door slammed shut and Danny tromped into the kitchen with an armload of books.

"Put those in the family room, sweetheart," Erica instructed him. "And then go wash up. That goes for everyone," she announced with the authority of a seasoned wife and mother. "Dinner is almost ready."

The setting sun's rays slanted across the porch as Erica rocked slowly back and forth on the porch swing. Sam and Danny had washed and dried the dishes without being asked, and the kitchen fairly sparkled with cleanliness. Both children were already in bed, as they were getting up at dawn to spend the day riding horses with the neighbors. The sounds of Will's shower reached Erica out on the porch, the old pipes bellowing in protest inside the walls.

Resting her feet on the porch rail, she thought back to the very first time she'd enjoyed the comforts of this swing.

They'd all become hopelessly entangled in one another's lives since that day. She drew a deep breath and expelled it slowly. Never in her wildest dreams had Erica ever thought she could fall so deeply in love with a man. And his children. And his rambling old farmhouse out in the middle of nowhere. This wasn't her style. No. She was a jet-setting up-and-comer who enjoyed the fabulous opportunities her wealthy patients afforded her. That's what she was ... not some farmer's wife.

Then why was it that she was sitting there completely miserable, wondering how she would ever be able to return to her previous life. A life that held no allure at all anymore. Well, she had no choice in that matter. Eventually— probably sooner than later—she would have to return to nursing.

Letting her head drop back on the swing, she stared at the porch ceiling. She would give anything to know what the future held. All this patient waiting was beginning to take its toll. Groaning, she squeezed her eyes tightly shut and willed the throbbing in her temples to subside. If only she could talk to Emily. If only she could be sure that her sister was all right. If only she could confess her sins and get rid of the guilt she'd carried from the moment she'd gazed into Will's stunning sea-green eyes. If only she knew whether or not Will would marry her sister ... then she could make plans. To leave the country. Forever. *If only, if only, if only...* echoed depressingly in her mind, until she thought she'd scream.

Lifting her head off the back of the swing, she opened her eyes and peered into the star-filled evening sky. That was the answer, she thought as she gazed up at the heavens. She would have to go live in a different country. Start over. Away from her sister and her sister's new family. The family she'd come to think of as her own.

The thought of being so far away from her twin tore at her heart. Not to mention the searing pain of being so far away from Will and the kids. But she would do it for their happiness. Because she loved them. All of them. With all her heart—what was left of it. Hearing the screen door bounce shut, she tried to shake off her melancholy and smile at Will.

"Hi."

He greeted her in the same sexy, low voice she'd loved from the moment she'd first heard it.

"You can't sit out here on the sweetheart swing without your sweetheart."

He settled down beside her. "Didn't you know that?" he teased, putting his arm around her shoulders and squeezing gently. He smelled of soap and after-shave and . . . Will. Erica wanted to cry.

"I take it you're volunteering for the job." She smiled up at him. A bittersweet longing filled her and left a stinging sensation behind her eyes.

"I could be persuaded," he said softly, and kissed her lightly on the lips. He shifted on the swing and drew her more firmly into his arms. Looking deeply into her eyes, he said, "If the truth were known, I could be persuaded to be far more than your sweetheart." He cupped her chin in the palm of his hand and bent his head to hers. His kiss was featherlight, and soft as the morning dew. Even so, it once again succeeded in driving all rational thought from Erica's mind.

"Yeah?" she whispered against his lips.

"Yeah." He sighed and deepened their kiss.

The old porch swing creaked and groaned, swaying with their movements. A light breeze rustled the leaves on the hazelnut trees, carrying their soft sigh through the warm summer evening.

Will summoned every ounce of strength he possessed and pulled his mouth from hers. His voice hoarse, he said, "Before we go any further here, there's something I want to ask you."

"Yeah?" she asked hazily, still clutching the front of his cotton shirt in her fingers.

"Yeah." He grinned and gently pried her fingers from his shirt, and held her hands in his. "I've been giving some very serious thought to my future lately."

Erica stared blankly at him, her mind still muzzy from his kiss.

"Not just my future, actually. The kids', too. And—" he smoothed an errant lock of hair out of her glassy eyes "—yours."

"Mine?"

"Yours."

It was beginning to dawn on Erica where Will was heading, and her stomach clenched in fear. She had to stop him. But how? She could say she thought she saw a bear run through the orchard. Or, even more distracting, she could run bare through the orchard herself. Her mind raced with the wild possibilities, none of which seemed right. While Erica frantically racked her brain for solutions to this predicament, Will continued shyly.

"And the more I think about my future—" he smiled tenderly and lifted her hand to his mouth for a kiss "—the less I can envision it without you."

"Me?" she squeaked. No. Emily. You mean Emily, she thought wildly.

"You."

"Surely there are other nannies out there who could fill your needs," she hedged, grasping at straws.

He looked puzzled for a moment and then broke into a wide smile. "I'm not asking you to stay on as our nanny."

"No?" she croaked.

"No."

"Oh." Stall him! her mind screamed.

"Sweetheart, what I'm trying to do... Oh, this is coming out badly," he said, and rubbed her hand across his jaw in frustration.

Faint! Scream! Run! Something . . . anything. Just don't let him ask. Unfortunately, while Erica wrestled with her plan of action, Will got down to the point of the matter.

Sliding off the swing, he dropped to the porch on one knee. His crooked smile was full of tenderhearted hope, as he took her hand in his. "Ms. Brant," he began.

"Yes?" Erica whispered, filled with the wonder—and terror—of it all.

"Would you do me the honor of becoming Mrs. Will Spencer?"

Her mouth dropped open in shock. It was one thing to wonder what his proposal would be like. It was another thing entirely to hear the actual words. Mixed shivers ran down her spine. Shivers of trepidation and anticipation.

As if afraid she might turn down his proposal before she had time to weigh the benefits, he hurriedly continued, "I love you, sweetheart." Using her hand, he pulled himself back up into the swing. "And I want you to stay with me and the kids—if you'll have us. I know they love you almost as much as I do."

"Oh, Will," she murmured, touched to the point of tears. The frustration of the situation was rapidly approaching unbearable. The innocent hope reflected in his eyes tore at her heart. What could she possibly answer that wouldn't hurt someone?

Just as she opened her mouth to reply to Will's earnest request, something happened that would change Erica's life. Just as she began to blurt out that she would love to become Mrs. Will Spencer, just as she lifted her face to his for the mind-boggling kiss that would surely follow—the phone rang.

At first, neither one moved. Then, realizing that she'd just been thrown a lifeline back to reality, Erica leaped to her feet. Will stared at her retreating back in surprise as he swayed to and fro in the swing she'd so rapidly evacuated.

"I'll get it," she called as the screen door banged shut.

Will sighed and settled low in the seat. First thing tomorrow he was going to call the phone company and have his service cut off, he thought grumpily.

Erica answered the phone to find it was Emily on the line. After all this time and worry, the prodigal sister was finally phoning home. The timing was uncanny. Was this some kind of omen? She had been in the process of agreeing to marry her sister's man. The only reason she'd agreed to this fiasco in the first place was to help Emily land a husband. And here she was, on the verge of stealing him for herself. How depraved! How selfish! How could she ever look herself in the mirror again? The sound of Emily's perky voice filled her with guilt. And anger.

"Where on earth have you been?" Erica demanded, looking over he shoulder to make sure Will hadn't followed her into the house.

"At home," she said cheerfully, as though that should be obvious. "I just got back this morning and I have so much to tell you!" she bubbled enthusiastically.

"Well, I have a thing or two to tell you, too," Erica declared in agitation—anxious to spill the speech she'd been rehearsing for days—before Will came in and overheard their conversation.

"How'd it go?" Emily asked curiously. "Did he figure out that you're not me?"

"No," Erica huffed impatiently. "In fact, it went well. Too well. That's why you're getting your little derriere back here tomorrow. I can't take this anymore," she cried, near tears. "I'm leaving first thing tomorrow morning. It's my turn to disappear. I need a vacation, to...sort things out. So I'm going away for a few days. I don't know where, so don't try to find me," she threatened. "Just get here fast." After weeks of longing to spill her guts to her sister, she suddenly knew that she just couldn't. Not now. Not on the phone. Her poor sister deserved better than to come home after a grueling summer in the trenches with the homeless and find out that her evil twin had stolen her man. Erica's face burned with shame. She didn't deserve to live.

"But, Erica. Wait. I have some important news I wanted to tell you. I can't come back. Something came up and..."

"What?" Erica practically shrieked into the mouth-piece. "You can't do this to me." There was no way she could stay here under the same roof for another day, engaged to marry her future brother-in-law.

"Erica, if you would just listen to me for a second—"

"No!" Erica shouted. "You listen to me. We had a deal. I've held up my end of this charade. Now, you come and take over your responsibility to your future family the way you promised."

"But, Erica, you don't understand. They're not my fut—"

Blood boiling, Erica cut her off. "I understand perfectly," she said sweetly into the mouthpiece. "You have some other rainbow you want to chase before you settle down. Well, not this time. The answer is no."

Emily persistently tried to get her twin to listen to reason.

"That's what I've been trying to tell you. I'm through chasing rainbows, as you put it. I'm ready to settle down and be a wife and mother. Really. Right now. But there is something I have to tell you first."

Even though she didn't turn around to make certain, Erica could feel Will's presence in the room. Smiling brittlely, she glanced up at him and spoke sweetly to her sister.

"I'm sure you can explain it all when I see you. I'll leave first thing tomorrow morning, so you'll need to *make arrangements for yourself as soon as possible.*" She prayed that Emily got the message.

"But," Emily sputtered.

"No buts now. I won't hear of anything else. I'll see you when I see you," Erica said firmly. "Until then, good luck." She was unconscious of the tears that streamed down her face as she hung up on her protesting sister and switched the phone's ringer off. Emily might try to call back.

"Is everything all right?" Will asked, standing uncertainly in the doorway, eyeing her tear-stained face with concern.

Sending him a watery smile, she swiped at her eyes with the side of her hand. "I'm fine." She nodded. "That was my...mom...again...there," she said, referring to the last time he'd caught her on the phone. "I have to go to her...tomorrow...early. She's, um, having some more..." Erica sniffed, her face crumpling as the realization that Emily was really back hit her. "Health problems," she blubbered.

"Oh, sweetheart." Will strode across the room and pulled her into his comforting embrace. "I'm so sorry," he murmured, and stroked her hair. She seemed too overcome with emotion to elaborate, so he didn't press. When the time was right, she would explain, he was sure.

"I should go pack," she whispered forlornly into his shirt.

"Of course." Will kissed her forehead. "Go home and take care of business. I'm sure we can manage for a day or two without you. But—" his voice was rough with his need for her "—hurry back, sweetheart. We'll miss you. Especially me."

Erica nodded, stunned with grief. "Uh, I, uh...should be back soon," she stammered, hoping against hope that her birdbrained sister would arrive on schedule to pick up the threads of this ruse.

"Take your time, honey. Really. We'll live." He kneaded the knots in the back of her neck with loving fingers. "I'll miss you like crazy, though."

Erica nodded and drew in a sad, shuddered breath. Leaving Will was a million times worse than she'd ever dreamed it could be. And she hadn't even *started* grieving over the kids. Why did life have to be so complicated?

"I'll miss you, too." Eyes flashing, Erica stared at Will, drinking in every subtle detail of his beautiful face. Someday, when she was an elderly spinster, she would cherish these memories.

The next morning at the crack of dawn, Erica dragged herself and her suitcases downstairs to the kitchen. Her face was red and blotchy and her eyes were swollen from the gallons of tears she'd cried all night long. Sitting by the window, she'd gazed morosely out into the star-filled night, waiting for an answer, a sense of peace to wash over her, telling her that she was doing the right thing by leaving. The feeling never came. Instead she'd felt the distant stars mock her, and weary with unimaginable grief, she'd finally gone to bed and drifted into a fitful sleep.

In the kitchen Will was waiting for her, a pot of strong, aromatic coffee perking on the counter. He looked up in surprise as Erica entered the room, her face revealing the ravages of her restless, pain-filled night. Obviously the situation with her mother was much more serious than she'd let on. Will poured her a cup of coffee and joined her at the table.

"As soon as you finish your coffee, I'll drive you into Harvest Valley to the bus station," he told her.

"No." She smiled wanly at his sweet suggestion, uttered in that loving-husband voice she was growing to fear she couldn't live without. "The kids will be getting up soon. They're going riding with the neighbors, remember? I already called a cab. It should be here any minute."

"Oh." He felt strangely depressed. "I was hoping to spend some time with you this morning."

"I know," she said, and was glad she'd called the cab for exactly that reason. She couldn't stand to prolong the agony any longer.

Will took a sip of his coffee. "I should go wake up the kids, then. They'll want to say goodbye."

"No, no. Let them sleep. Really."

"But they have to get up anyway," he protested.

"Oh, Will, I'll be back before you know it." She crossed her fingers behind her back. There was no way she could stand saying goodbye to the kids too. She'd lose it for sure.

"Well, okay," he said, finally capitulating.

A car horn sounded sharply through the kitchen window.

"That's my ride," she said unnecessarily. They stood up and faced each other awkwardly for a moment.

"I'll get your bags." Will took a step, but before he could reach her luggage, Erica threw herself into his arms.

Reaching up, she pulled his face down to hers and kissed him hard. Almost desperately. Knowing it would be their last kiss left an incredible ache in her heart, and she clung to him, feverishly kissing his cheeks, his eyes, his throat and, once more, his lips.

"Goodbye," she whispered as the car horn sounded again. With one last urgent kiss, Erica picked up her bags and ran to the cab before Will could protest.

"Drive," she ordered the cabbie, and without a backward glance, disappeared from Will's life.

Chapter Eleven

Erica dialed Will's number and anxiously waited for someone to pick up the phone. Finally, on the fourth ring, she heard her sister's breathy "Hello?"

"You're there. Good." Erica sighed with relief.

"Yes. I'm here," Emily replied. "Where are you?"

"I'm at the coast till tomorrow. Then I'll go back to our place and start job hunting. I've been thinking about looking for something overseas."

"You have? Why?"

"I need to get away." And the farther away the better, she thought gloomily. Just knowing that Emily was standing in Will's house, talking on Will's phone, caused a painful twisting in Erica's gut. "How are they?" she asked, her voice barely above a whisper.

"I don't know. I just got here, and nobody's home. The back door was open."

"You might check the barn. Sometimes . . ." Erica tried

to speak past the growing lump in her throat. "Sometimes the kids go out there and keep Will company."

"Okay, I'll do that." Emily sounded distracted. "Now, Erica, I have something I need to discuss with you. It's very important. I've been trying to tell you since I got back. It's about... Will and me."

The last thing Erica wanted to hear about at this point was her sister's relationship with Will. She was in far too much pain for that now. Maybe in a few weeks, when she had a permanent job nailed down, she could listen to her sister babble on happily about the little pleasures of her relationship with Will. Later. Right now, it was still too soon.

"And I want to hear every juicy detail. Really I do," she lied, feeling nauseated at the thought. "Unfortunately I have to leave now. I'm... having dinner with friends. I'll call you." Maybe then, she could finally bare her soul to Emily and confess her illicit love for Will. On the other hand, that might not be such a bright idea. Head throbbing, she knew she was making herself sick with guilt and indecision.

"But," Emily cried in frustration.

"And, Em?" she cut her sister off. "You'd better take good care of that family or," she warned grimly, "I'll know the reason why." And with that sage, though somewhat threatening, piece of advice, Erica hung up.

"Wow. You got your hair cut." The disappointment was evident in Will's voice as he entered the kitchen. The kids came tramping in right behind him.

"Oh. Uh, yes," Emily replied, touching her chic bob. "Where have you been?"

"In the barn," Will answered cautiously, wondering why he felt a sudden coolness coming from her. He'd been looking forward to her arrival for two long days, and now that she was here, it felt as if they were complete strangers.

Crossing over to the sink, he decided to wash up before taking her in his arms.

The kids stopped suddenly and stood staring strangely at Emily, as though they were seeing her now for the first time.

"Hi," she said uneasily.

Sam crossed the kitchen floor to stand immediately in front of Emily. She peered intently up at her nanny, until a broad smile broke over her face.

"You're not her," she announced, puzzled but delighted by her find.

"I'm not who?" Emily asked.

"You're not Emily."

"Oh. Well . . . actually, I am Emily. But in a way you're right."

Sam squinted up at Emily, her arms folded thoughtfully over her chest. "You sure look like her, though. Are you guys twins or something?" Glancing around behind Emily, she wondered aloud, "Where is she, anyway?"

Drying his hands on a dish towel, a very confused Will turned around to look at his daughter and this woman he thought he knew so well. "Would someone mind telling me what's going on?" He glanced quickly back and forth between the two.

"I don't think she's our nanny, Dad," Danny announced, shaking his head warily.

"What do you mean she's not your nanny, son? Just because someone gets her hair cut, doesn't mean she's not the same person anymore. Does it?" He laughed nervously and gazed quizzically at Emily. "Does it?" He repeated, not so sure anymore himself.

"Why don't we all sit down here at the kitchen table," Emily suggested with a shaky laugh. "I've got an amusing little story to tell you."

* * *

Will was not amused. In fact, he'd never been angrier in his life. He'd been duped by a couple of scheming women, and he was mad as hell about it. Before Emily had even gotten halfway through her incredible story, Will had heard enough. Not waiting to sit through every detail of the disgusting, sordid tale, he'd stormed out of the house to take refuge in the barn.

"Women," he muttered, his voice harsh with hurt, and savagely threw his hammer across the vast interior of the barn. Why hadn't Emily just told him the truth in the first place? He would have understood... eventually. And what about her twin? Erica, wasn't it? Why had someone he was so sure was sensible and levelheaded gone along with such a stupid plan? He felt like a first-class fool.

Temper flaring, Will decided it was time for that spring housecleaning he'd been putting off for months, and proceeded to tear the insides of the barn completely apart.

"Dad?" Sam called tentatively into the shadowed cavernous barn.

"What are you still doing up? It's way past your bedtime. Go back in the house."

"But, Dad... I wanted to tell you what Emily said." Clad only in her summer nightie, she tiptoed barefoot into the barn, searching for her father among the wreakage.

"I don't care what she said," Will barked, livid all over again. "Get out of here, and go to bed now."

"But, Dad! She said a bunch of stuff that you should know. Stuff that would help you understand what's going on." Sam's pleading only served to further infuriate Will.

"I understand everything I want or need to know. Now—" his voice dropped to an ominous level "—so help me, Sam, if you're not in bed by the time I count five, there will be hell to pay." He threw a wrench into his toolbox to punctuate his fury.

Too stunned and hurt to shed the tears that burned in her eyes, Sam turned and fled to the safety of the house.

"There will be hell to pay," Sam whispered to herself as she sat on the stoop of Erica's San Francisco apartment and waited for her to come home. Luckily, she didn't have long to wait.

"Sam? Is that you?" Erica asked, incredulous at finding the thirteen-year-old girl so far from home. "Where's your dad?" She studied the girl's pinched and drawn expression. It was obvious she'd spent some time in tears.

Sam sighed. "At home. I ran away."

Her heart lurching violently, Erica cried, *"You what?"* She shifted her packages in her arms and, fishing her keys out of her pocket, opened her front door. "Come inside, honey, and tell me what's going on."

Following Erica into the Victorian apartment she shared with Emily, Sam went into the living room and slumped dejectedly on the sofa.

"How did you get here?" Erica called from the kitchen, where she deposited her bags. Something was wrong. She leaned against the kitchen counter to steady her wobbly legs. What exactly did the girl know? she wondered. She didn't want to ruin Emily's chances with Will by blurting out the truth. On the other hand, she was sick to death of all the lies.

"The bus."

"Who gave you the money?"

"I used my savings."

"Sam." Shaking her head in disbelief, Erica came into the living room and sat down next to Sam. "How did you know where to g' San Francisco is a big place."

"I found your address in her purse." Sam looked her square in the eye. "Emily's purse."

"Ah" was the only response Erica was capable of at the moment. Much to Erica's further consternation, Sam promptly burst into tears.

"I know who you are. Emily told us everything," she said between the fits and starts of her emotional storm.

"She did?" Erica was completely nonplussed. Why would she do something like that? None of this made any sense. But then, when had anything Emily had ever done made any sense?

"Yes." Sam nodded emphatically, her raven mop falling into her red and puffy eyes completely unnoticed. She tried valiantly, her breathing labored and erratic, to choke out what was bothering her. "Why did you leave us? You broke my dad's heart. Just like—" she pulled her lower lip into her mouth and stared at Erica with accusing, red-rimmed eyes "—when my mom died. He loves you. And I thought you were starting to love him, too. And Danny and me." She buried her head in her hands, her whole body shaking with emotion. "I thought I finally had a real mom."

Erica felt like the lowest form of life on the planet as she gathered the sobbing child into her arms and smoothed her hair away from her face.

"Oh, Sam. I know that after the crazy stunt my sister and I pulled on you guys you'll have a hard time believing anything I say, but I do love you. Very much. Danny, too. And I love your dad. But don't you see, honey? It can never be. I lied to your father about who I was all summer long. And even worse than that, by falling in love with your dad and you kids, I betrayed my twin sister's trust. You see...she loves your dad, too."

Sam shook her head violently. "She does not!"

"Yes, she does, sweetheart. That's why I came to live with you guys in the first place. She loved your dad and wanted—"

"No!" Sam interrupted emphatically. "Really, Em—I mean Erica. She *doesn't!* She told us that when she was—"

Before Sam could finish her thought, the doorbell rang.

"Here." Erica plucked a couple of tissues from the box on the coffee table and handed them to Sam. Patting her on the knee, she reassured her, "I'll get rid of whoever that is and be right back. Then I think it would be a good idea if we called your father to tell him where you are. He must be absolutely frantic with worry." The doorbell rang again, this time more insistently.

Sam smiled weakly. "Okay, but I left a note, so he's probably not too worried."

"That's good," she said, nodding at the girl. "Hold your horses," she groused at the thoughtless goon who was leaning on her doorbell.

She was sure her heart stopped beating as she pulled the door open to find Will standing on the stoop with Emily and Danny. They all looked so wonderful to her heartsick eyes she just stood for a moment, unmoving, drinking in the small group she loved so well, despite the pain it cost.

"You're here," she breathed, stunned.

"Sam?" There were dark circles of worry under Will's eyes.

"Yes." Nodding, Erica moved back to let them into the apartment. Will wasted no time in reaching his daughter and sweeping her tightly into his arms. Curious, Danny followed to observe the eventual punishment, leaving Erica and Emily standing alone in the foyer.

Still in shock at the amazing turn of events, Erica reached up and touched Emily's new bob.

"Your hair!"

"It's a very long, very involved story." Emily grinned and ran her fingers through her short, stylish cut. "One I've been trying to tell you for days now. However, it's a story, after having spent all night talking to Will, that I think he should tell you himself."

Erica's heart landed in her shoes. Unable to say anything, for fear she'd make a complete fool out of herself, she merely nodded.

"So—" Emily peeked over her sister's shoulder into the living room "—I'm going to grab the kids and take them out for some ice cream at Ghiradelli Square. You and Will have some unresolved business, according to him. Plus, since I can't seem to get a word in edgewise with you, I'll let him tell you about the engagement."

It was then Erica noticed the gigantic diamond engagement ring that adorned her twin's slender left hand. Blinking rapidly to stem the flow of tears that threatened, Erica could only nod dumbly again, a sickly smile permanently tattooed to her face. They were engaged. The reality was even worse than the speculation she'd been doing for days.

"Hey, you two," Emily called to the kids. "Hot fudge sundaes on me. Get a move on, now. We've got ice cream to eat." As the kids grabbed their sweaters, Emily turned to Will. "Take your time." She smiled and pecked him on the cheek. "We may even head to Alcatraz for a while. Fisherman's Wharf, too." Grinning, she winked at him and, taking each child firmly in hand, disappeared through the front door.

Erica stood in the living room archway and stared out into the foyer in disbelief. Will's voice pulled her attention over to the sofa, where he sat, motioning for her to join him.

"Why did you leave?" he asked, his voice raw with emotion.

Oh, how she was dreading this conversation. Well, she decided, better to bite the bullet and get it over with once and for all than to go through this torture any longer. Best just to plunge right in. She perched next to him on the sofa and studied her hands as though she'd never seen them before.

"Because I love you."

"You love me and then you leave. What is that?"

"I left because Emily loves you, and she loved you first."

"Yeah." Will snorted. "She told me."

Suddenly Erica was irritated. "Well, you certainly didn't waste any time proposing to her."

Will raked his fingers through his hair in exasperation and cursed under his breath. "I didn't propose to her. I proposed to you. You're the one I love. You're the one I want."

Confused, Erica stared blankly at Will. "But what about Emily? What about your engagement. I, uh," she stammered, "I saw the ring."

Will grinned, beginning to see the humor in the situation now that he was back with the woman he loved. Last night Emily had gone out to the barn after Sam had gone to bed. For hours, they'd sat drinking coffee out of a thermos she'd prepared, while she'd explained everything to Will. How this whole crazy farce had been her idea, how she'd manipulated Erica into going along with it and how she'd spent her summer researching her thesis.

"Well, it seems our Emily wasn't so infatuated with me after all, and has fallen in love with her boss down in L.A."

"Her boss?"

"Trust me when I tell you it's a very long, very wacky story, and a situation that only your sister could get herself into." Will smiled an amused, brotherly smile and took Erica's hand in his. "Anyway, when I told her that we'd fallen in love, she was thrilled for us. She explained that she had twisted your arm and blackmailed you emotionally to get your help this summer. And while I don't approve of your methods, your motives were pure."

Erica stared at him, agog with the wonder of his words.

Pulling a booted foot up over his knee, he turned on the sofa to face Erica. "You know, it still boggles my mind that I couldn't tell the difference between you two right away. You are about as different as night and day. All I can say is, I probably never would have looked twice at Emily. I never felt anything for her, and that's the honest truth, until you came back from San Francisco, instead of her. Then—" he laughed at the irony "—the attraction I felt for you hit me like a tote of hazelnuts. There is just something magic about you for me." He kissed the delicate fingertips he held in his hand. "For the kids, too."

Finally finding her voice, Erica asked, "You mean you can forgive me?"

"I already have."

Her eyes bright with emotion, she looked into Will's warm gaze and smiled with relief at the love she saw reflected there. "Oh, Will," she whispered, too choked up to say any more.

Drawing her into his lap, Will put his arms around her waist and squeezed. "Emily—uh, sorry—" he grinned sheepishly "—force of habit. Erica, my kids love you almost as much as I do, and none of us can envision life without you. So, if it's okay with you, we'd all like to marry you."

Eyes flashing with hope and joy, Erica took his wonderful, handsome face in her hands and gently kissed his crooked smile. "Yes, Will Spencer. I will marry you and your children."

Overcome with relief, Will pulled his fiancée's lips down to his and kissed her with a passion that would have sent Huck howling from the room.

"You know," he said, running his hands through the long hair he loved so much, "history is repeating itself."

"What do you mean?" Erica stopped kissing his ear long enough to ask.

"Well, July had a crush on me before I met June."

Erica stopped what she was doing and giggled. "Really?"

"Yeah, but once she met Charlie, I was left in the dust. Kind of like Emily," he mused in mock sadness.

"Lucky for June and me," she said cheekily, and kissed him along his jaw. "Will you be all right?"

"Umm," he growled, and pushed her back against the arm of the sofa. "Just keep it up. With you to nurse me back, I should recover nicely."

* * * * *

And the SISTER SWITCH continues....
Don't miss the fun as Emily finds
her own man to love
in Weekend Wife, *available in May—*
only from Silhouette Romance.

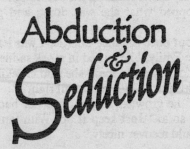

THIS SIDE OF HEAVEN

The miracle of love is waiting to be discovered
in Duncan, Oklahoma! Arlene James takes you there
in her miniseries, THIS SIDE OF HEAVEN.
Look for book four in February:

THE ROGUE WHO CAME TO STAY

Rodeo champ Griff Shaw had come home to Duncan to heal when he
found pretty single mom Joan Burton and her adorable daughter
living in his house! Griff wasn't about to turn Joan and her little girl
out, but did Joan dare share a roof with this rugged rogue?

Available in February, from

🖋️ *Silhouette* ROMANCE™

WHERE THE HEART IS

Don't miss the final book in
this heartwarming series from

ELIZABETH AUGUST

A HUSBAND FOR SARAH

Sam Raven had teased and challenged Sarah Orman as a girl, now he dared her to accept his wild proposal. Would Sarah's lifelong rival become her lifetime love?

WHERE THE HEART IS: With her wit and down-to-earth charm, Sarah Orman always had a way of bringing couples together. Now she finds a romance of her own!

Available in March, only from

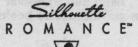

Silhouette
R O M A N C E™

This March rediscover
a forgotten love with

by *Request*™

missing
memories

Is the power of love strong enough to bring back a past that has
been forgotten?

Three complete novels by your favorite authors—in one special
collection!

TALL IN THE SADDLE by Mary Lynn Baxter
FORGOTTEN DREAM by Paula Detmer Riggs
HAWK'S FLIGHT by Annette Broadrick

The path to love can be treacherous...especially if you don't
remember the way!

**Available wherever
Harlequin and Silhouette books are sold.**

HARLEQUIN®   *Silhouette*®